THE OORT PLAGUE
A Pandemic Apocalypse

I0738015

Creative Texts Publishers products are available at special discounts for bulk purchase for sale promotions, premiums, fund-raising, and educational needs. For details, write Creative Texts Publishers, PO Box 50, Barto, PA 19504, or visit www.creativetexts.com

THE OORT PLAGUE: A PANDEMIC APOCALYPSE
Book Two of The Oort Chronicles
Published by Creative Texts Publishers
PO Box 50
Barto, PA 19504
www.creativetexts.com

Copyright 2018 by Cliff Deane
All rights reserved

Cover design copyright 2019 Creative Texts Publishers, LLC

This book or parts thereof may not be reproduced in any form, stored in a retrieval system, or transmitted in any form by any means—electronic, mechanical, photocopy, recording, or otherwise—without prior written permission of the publisher, except as provided by United States of America copyright law.

The following is a work of fiction. Any resemblance to actual names, persons, businesses, and incidents is strictly coincidental. Locations are used only in the general sense and do not represent the real place in actuality.

ISBN: 978-0-578-49732-7

THE OORT PLAGUE
A Pandemic Apocalypse

BY CLIFF DEANE

CREATIVE TEXTS PUBLISHERS
Barto, Pennsylvania

This book is dedicated to Mrs. Eileen Nearing Greene,
a dear friend of more than fifty years.

A Note to My Readers

The science behind the premise of this book is accurate.

I surely hope you enjoy reading

<u>The Oort Plague</u>
A Pandemic Apocalypse

It is estimated that as many as two-trillion comets still reside in the Oort Cloud, which is the farthest known limit of our Solar System.

CONTENTS

THE SCIENCE STUFF

The Oort Cloud

The Star System named Sol

It is estimated that as many as two-trillion comets still reside in the Oort Cloud, which is the farthest known limit of our Solar System.

The distance is so great that a number written in miles would have absolutely no meaning, even to Astronomers. To create a measurable distance, Scientists now use a term called the AU (Astronomical Unit). One AU is equal to the distance from the Earth to the Sun, some ninety-three million miles. In math notation that would be 93,000,000, and since the Oort Cloud measures out to as much as ten-thousand AUs, using the number nine-hundred and thirty billion miles becomes incomprehensible.

The Holly Thorne Comet began its descent toward the Sun after being struck by, and fused with, several other dirty snowballs. These collisions sent the now huge comet tumbling out of the Oort. As she began falling toward Sol, Holly Thorne picked up other small comets. She now measured thirty miles across. The series of glancing blows created a wobbling rotation.

The voyage of Holly would take two-thousand three-hundred, and fifty-nine years from the time it began to plummet toward Sol. The birth of Jesus Christ was still three-hundred and fifty years in the Earth's future.

CHAPTER ONE

A Chain is only as Strong as its Weakest Link

7 MARCH 2118
PRESIDENT GREENE
MOUNT WEATHER

Sitting behind a two-hundred-year-old walnut desk, President Eileen N. Greene quietly listened to her closest advisors, her Chief of Staff retired Three Star General Harry Wolfe, NASA Director Gordon Winters, The Chairman of the Joint Chiefs, Four Star General H. H. (Triple H) Howard, and Homeland Security Chief Mack Holland.

These wise men were in her office twenty minutes before the full Comet Committee met to convince the President that she should utilize the brain power of those men to come up with a way to tell the American people what to expect in the coming days.

The President entered the Presidential Conference Room in the Mount Weather facility following her Chief of Staff (COS). The committee members quickly stood and waited for President Greene to take her place at the head of the table and direct these trusted friends to take their seats.

"Gentlemen, please be seated," said the President. She then gaveled the meeting into session. As was her normal procedure, Greene wasted no time in getting down to business.

"My friends, I wish to pick your brains to allow me to appropriately address the nation, warning them of the coming pandemic. I had, at first, considered telling our citizens about the devolution of so many of our citizens into Mags. But, after considerable thought, I have decided to keep that information under wraps until the pandemic has run its course. At that point, I will inform them of the tragedy aboard our mining vessels and recommend that everyone go armed. Explaining why will be difficult, but it must be done. Today, however, we will discuss the speech I must give this evening at 7:00 pm."

The discussions lasted for over an hour before each member had provided their individual take on what, and how, the President would say to the nation.

After this consultation with the Comet Committee, President Greene believed, given the situation, that she had the best possible wording to address the American people.

7 MARCH 2118, 1900
PRESIDENT GREENE
MOUNT WEATHER

"My fellow Americans, I have received word from the CDC that they have detected a new and serious virus which has somehow found its way into the three mining vessels, infecting the heroic crews which were so successful in altering the course of Comet Holly Thorne. This virus has suddenly attacked the three crews with severe flu-like symptoms. Initial evidence indicates that this virus came from the comet and entered the ships through the hull breaches caused by the nuclear attack upon Holly Thorne by the SRI-Federation.

"The CDC has recommended that over the next few days everyone should stock up on sufficient foodstuffs to last for two-weeks. The CDC suggests that the foods you purchase should be those that are easily eaten and digested, like bread, jello, and pudding. They also suggest that you stock up on painkillers, such as Tylenol and large doses of vitamins, especially vitamin C. The Head of the CDC, Doctor Tyler Deen also recommends anti-diarrheal and anti-vomiting meds.

"At this point, it is unknown if the preparations will actually be needed, but it is better to have these items and not need them. Should you become ill with flu-like symptoms, do not plan on going to the hospital, or your family Doctor, as they may also be incapacitated.

"My friends, I would prefer that this warning was not needed, but the CDC believes that this new virus has been brought to us by the comet Holly Thorne.

"Please, I urge you not to panic. Don't purchase more of the recommended supplies than you will need for your families. If we remain calm, then things may well return to normal after ten days, or so. Remember, if you hoard, others may die as a result of your personal greed."

Within hours of this outpouring of news, members of the government began showing up at every governmental bunker they could reach.

7 MARCH 2118
DIG SITE
MOUNDSVILLE, WV

Jake gathered all his dig team together and managed to calm the panic that was rising in his student's minds, like acid-reflux after a spicy Pakistani meal.

He said, "Okay, I need for everyone to take a deep breath through the nose and exhale it out of your toes." Surprisingly, this helped with the initial fear. Jake continued by assigning tasks to each group of three. He decided to send two males with each female. The teams were each assigned to purchase the appropriate quantity of each of the items suggested by the CDC and added copious amounts of water.

The individuals of each group were told to take their knives used in the digging process. Those who had no knives were given sharpened Phillip's head screwdrivers. Jake didn't think the rioting would begin before tomorrow, but he wanted each team member to be as well protected as possible. Jake was also pleasantly surprised to discover that, as many of the dig team were West Virginians, most of the men and two of the women had firearms stored in their gear.

Before they departed on their team missions, Jake said, "If you are in a store which sells ammunition, buy as much as they will sell. Even more importantly, emulate the Boy Scouts and Be Prepared for possible trouble. Don't start trouble but you must not hesitate to finish it if it comes your way."

For himself, Jake opened his footlocker and retrieved a 9 mm sidearm and holster. Gale, being one tough gal, also had a 9 mil in her locker. They both buckled up and looked at each other with happiness that they would be facing this mess together. Their eyes also betrayed their fear and dread of the coming days.

Each team set about their tasks and were surprised to discover that the panic buying had already started.

Team three, Frank Lusk, Donna Pritt, and David Brewer were sent to a Walmart Supercenter in Moundsville. When they arrived at the store, each member of the team could feel that the atmosphere around the store was charged with fear, worry, and determination.

Frank, a former Army Infantryman, said, "Dave, why don't you wait here with the truck. I just don't like these vibes. Let's not take the chance of losing our transportation.

"Keep an eye out and when you see us coming back, watch for this signal. If we are in danger and being followed, I will walk on Donna's right side. She will be pushing the cart. Seeing that, keep low and be prepared to shoot if we must. Can you do that? Shoot, I mean, if we are in danger?

"An important note here, Dave; don't get trigger happy and don't start shooting until you see me reach for my gun. If you see that, then let the lead fly."

"Yeah, okay, I guess. Frank, I'm not crazy about the idea, but if I have to, I will. Oh, damn, Frank, this is some scary stuff." responded Dave.

"Yep, it surely is, just remember that it's better to be alive than it is to be dead."

Donna's mouth took on a sarcastic upturn at the corners. She said, "Frank, aren't you being just a bit melodramatic? This is a Walmart in Moundsville, not the center of Chicago."

Frank just looked at Donna and said, "No, I am not. Now, come on let's go get what we need and get back to the site. This place is gonna blow, and sooner than I thought. I saw the exact thing in Berzerkistan just before everything went to hell."

Donna and Frank exited the truck and walked into the static-filled Walmart. People were buying everything they could reach. For many, it looked like they had no idea what they needed, so they were just buying everything. The first thing on Frank's list was ammunition.

Donna asked, "Frank, while you get the ammo, how about I start on the list Jake gave us?"

"No!" said Frank in a quiet, but firm voice. "We stay together. This place could erupt at any moment, and I don't want to have to search for you in the middle of a riot."

Fortunately, most people were interested in foodstuffs, but by tomorrow, ammunition would be on most people's minds. Since there was no limit on ammo purchases, Frank bought out the entire display case of 9 mil and caliber .40. He looked down at the boxes of ammo and said to Donna, "It just amazes me that with all the ways technology has advanced, the best way to protect ourselves is still with an explosion and a chemically propelled piece of lead."

Once the boxes of ammo were placed in bags and seated in the cart, the couple began working their way through the store to complete their mission of food, water, and medications.

Donna said, "Frank, we need hygiene products, TP, and, like, you know, girl stuff."

Frank agreed and added those necessary items to their carts. As they left the store, Frank, who, from his Army experience, always made good use of situational awareness noticed two men following them. This learned skill came in handy as he noticed two poorly dressed and dirty men following them to the truck.

"Donna, don't turn around to look. Two men are following us. When we get to the truck, they plan to steal our supplies."

Donna, of course, tried to turn to look, but Frank quickly placed his hand on her shoulder saying, "Damn it, Donna, I said not to look. So, here's the plan; when we get to the truck, I want you to take the cart and go to the opposite side. Put the engine between you and our visitors. Then stay out of sight. Can you do that?"

Donna was a bit vexed by Frank's ordering her around, but she decided to keep her mouth shut, at least for now. "Yes, I understand," she said.

Frank placed himself on Donna's right side and placed his left hand around her waist. When they got to the truck, Donna hurried to the opposite side of the engine block.

"Easy Dave, not yet, but be ready," said Frank to the rear window of the full cab Ram 1500, 4X4.

"Hold it right there," said a voice from behind Frank, who's right hand was already in his jacket pocket. He slowly wrapped his hand around the grip of his pistol.

Frank turned and saw the small pistol in the hands of the ragged man. "Hello, friend," said Frank, "why do you need that gun?"

"Oh, we just figgered that you would be less likely to whine and complain about givin' us this nice truck and the stuff in your cart. Ain't that a nice truck Delbert?"

Delbert just said, "Uh, huh."

Oh, yeah, we'll be takin' the pretty lady, too. Sweetie, you will love the party we're a'takin you to. Ain't that right Delbert?"

"Uh, huh, she sure is uh purty'un Tink."

7 MARCH 2118
MOUNT WEATHER

Outside of the Mount Weather facility, hundreds of members of the Legislative Branch began showing up and demanding entrance. A young Second Lieutenant, Calvin Dudley, was the Duty Officer on 7 March 2118. He reported to the Chief of Staff that many people with children were gathering outside the complex wanting to be let in.

"Sir," said the Duty Officer, there are women and children out there. Should we open the door and let them in? Maybe they haven't become infected, yet?"

The COS responded with, "Lieutenant, if we open that door, we all die. I know this is heartrending and seems horribly selfish, but that door will not be opened. I want you to turn off the video and audio systems. There is to be no communication with anyone outside this facility. Are we clear on this?"

The young Second Lieutenant Dudley was not happy, but he said, "Yes, sir, we are clear."

"Good," said the COS, "now, I want to watch as you turn off the audio and video to the outside world."

With that, Mount Weather went dark.

Second Lieutenant Dudley, however, could not get the images of the children just outside the door out of his mind. Ten hours later, at 0200 hours, he turned the audio and video back on. Again, his heart began breaking. Dudley decided that denying them entrance to the bunker was tantamount to the murder of innocent women and children. At 0300 hours, he drew his sidearm and walked to the giant blast door.

When he came to within four feet of the Specialist (E-4) on guard duty, a wild-eyed, Lieutenant Dudley raised his pistol and told the guard that he was going to allow the women and children that were just on the other side of that door into Mount Weather.

Specialist Mathers looked down the barrel of the 9 mm service pistol and felt true fear. He could see the sadness or possibly madness in the eyes of this Lieutenant. He said, "Sir, please put down your sidearm. I have been ordered to keep this door locked. If I open it, we will all die."

"Specialist," said Dudley, "if you don't open it, you will surely die right now. We cannot be a part of the murder of innocent women and their little children. Now, open the door!"

"Sir," said Mathers, "please, don't shoot. You must understand that the virus is out there, and even opening the door a crack will doom us all."

"You don't know that! You don't know that, at all! What we do know is that if we don't open the door, those people outside will absolutely die. I cannot be a participant in the murder of children. Now, open that door!"

7 MARCH 2118
WALMART
MOUNDSVILLE, WV

As the two assailants slowly approached the truck, Frank's hand closed upon the pistol grip of his weapon, and he raised his hand to shoot, but Dave fired first and dropped the man with the pistol, as his bullet tore a path through the assailant's lower abdomen. The would-be robber and murderer fell writhing to the ground, screaming in intense agony as he covered the hole in his stomach with blood-soaked hands.

The second man turned to run, but Frank calmly put a bullet squarely between his shoulder blades. Delbert fell in a heap. Frank then walked to the wounded assailant and placed a 9 mm round into Tink's temple, putting him out of his agony. For a few short seconds, blood pooled from both wounds, until the man's heartbeat its last and ended the flow of blood.

Dave shouted to Frank, "Come on, people are gathering around the front of the parking lot. Hurry up; let's roll!"

Frank quickly jumped into the passenger seat as Dave jammed the truck into reverse. They raced out of the side parking lot, around the back of the Walmart and onto a side street, turning away from the front side of the store.

"Oh my God! Frank," shouted Donna, "he was running away. You just deliberately murdered him."

Frank's eyes turned cold and hard as he said, "Donna, these men were going to murder Dave and me, and then they would have taken you, the pretty lady, along as a sex slave to be raped and traded for a hit of meth. Did you see the rotten teeth of both men?"

"Yes, I saw their teeth, so what, you can't kill a man for having bad teeth!" screamed Donna.

Frank said in a very calm and soothing voice, "Heavy meth users tend to develop rotten teeth. One guy with bad choppers, maybe, but two together equals meth heads. Donna, these men were thieves, rapists, and murderers who planned to kill us. Sure, that pig was running away, and if I had let him go, he would have done the same thing to someone else who might not be prepared to stand and fight. That man would lose his life, his goods, and his wife, and all because I failed to rid the world of that piece of pond scum.

"Sure, I shot and killed him, because he and his friend would have murdered Dave and me before turning on you. I shot the wounded Meth-head to put him out of his pain, or maybe just to shut him up. You decide. Would you rather they succeeded in their robbery and murder attempt?"

Now in tears, Donna said, "Frank, you don't know they would have killed anyone, do you?"

"Donna; think about it. They would have had to kill us to keep the police off their ass. We've got to get back to the dig. You can plead your case with Professor Abraham, and then decide whether you still want to hand us over to the cops. Is that reasonable?"

Donna was still upset and crying as she said, "I guess it will have to be okay, since I'm sure you won't drop by the Sheriff's Station and turn yourselves in, right?"

"Yeah, Donna, that's right. You should also realize that Dave saved you from being raped and becoming a sex slave."

She then looked at Dave and said, "Dave, I know you shot that man because he had a gun aimed at Frank, so you're probably in the clear. Frank, however, just murdered a man in cold blood. Are you okay with that?"

Dave was clearly torn and angry when he said, "Woman, you are such an idiot. Yeah, it's true that the guy Frank offed would not have gotten you, but an hour from now, he would have shot first and taken what he needed from someone else. Didn't you see how dirty he was and how messed up his clothes were?"

"Oh, please, Dave, all that man needed was a helping hand and a hug. If we had shared what we have, he would have probably been very nice."

Dave's mouth dropped open, but no words came out; finally, he just closed his mouth and turned around in the seat, refusing to speak to her any longer.

"Frank asked, "Donna, would you like for me to drop you off at the Sheriff's Office?"

Sarcastically, she said, "Yes, I would like that. Will you do it?"

"No," smiled Frank, "I just wanted to see exactly how gullible and stupid you really are. Don't worry though, if we come across any other bums, I'll drop you off so you can share with those poor misfortunates who just need a hug and some understanding. Oh, one more thing. You are also now a fugitive on the run, and I guarantee both Dave and I will make you out to be the mastermind. Whadaya say, Dave?"

"Oh, hell yes," said Dave, "She is definitely the Bonnie to our two Clydes." This shut Donna up, but she cried all the way back to the dig site.

7 MARCH 2118
MOUNT WEATHER

Standing before the giant blast door, Specialist Mathers pleaded with Dudley, "Lieutenant, please, you know I can't open the door. I have my orders from the President."

At this point, Specialist Mathers hit the alarm button and then quickly lunged at Second Lieutenant Dudley, in an attempt to take his sidearm. In the short struggle which ensued, Specialist Mathers was shot in the left kidney.

Moving quickly, to get the door open before the alarm and shot brought the guard reaction force, Lieutenant Dudley pushed the lever which engaged the door. He allowed it to open only eighteen inches and shouted for the children to be put through.

Five young children made it through the door before the reaction force arrived and as Dudley turned to fire at the reinforcements, he was killed in a hail of gunfire.

The reaction force immediately shut the door and called the Officer of the Guard, who sent word up the line about the incident.

7 MARCH 2118
DIG SITE
MOUNDSVILLE, WV

Once each team had been dispatched on their various and sundry missions, Jacob contacted the University's PR section. PR then contacted the Moundsville National Guard Group Commander's Office. They were able to arrange for the Dig Team to set up in the Moundsville National Guard Armory's Training Room, which was large enough for the entire team to stay, in relative comfort. They could take up their temporary residence on the 13th of March.

Back at the dig site, Jacob and Gale were packing up their personal items for their stay at the Armory.

When Frank's team returned from the Walmart, Donna jumped out of the truck and ran to tell Jacob how Frank had murdered some poor, hungry man that just wanted a little help. She screamed, "Frank shot him in the back as he was trying to run away. We have to contact the Sheriff and have Frank arrested! Professor Abraham, quick, grab him before he murders us all!"

Frank calmly walked up to Jacob and Donna. He reached into his pocket and took out his pistol. He handed it over to Jacob, just as Dave came running up to be a part of the meeting.

Frank smiled and said, "Sir, would you like to hear my side of this now?"

After hearing what both Frank and Dave had to say, Jacob turned to Donna and asked, "Donna, is what these two men just said true?"

Crying now, Donna said, "Well, yes, but he just shot that poor man in the back, he was only trying to get away. Frank's a murderer!"

Jacob's voice took on an icy tone as he said, "Donna, I told you all, before you left, to be prepared for trouble and to handle it, doing whatever it took. Those two men wanted to kill both Frank and Dave, and then take everything, including you. By ridding the Earth of those vermin, Frank and Dave have saved the lives of other innocents. But, having said that, I'll make you a promise. The government says the pandemic will begin in another four or five days. If that doesn't happen, then I will personally drive you to the Sheriff's Office. Deal?"

"No, that is a terrible deal, but since you made us leave our cell phones in your office, I have no way of contacting the Police, I guess I'll have to go along with it." She then turned and ran to her tent.

Everyone on the team was enthusiastic about moving into the Guard Armory, well, everyone except Donna. She resented being forced to be quarantined inside an Army Fort where they planned how to kill innocent people. She actually hated the Armory more than she disliked being forced to share living space in mixed company, and she really hated that.

Jacob heard her whining and bitching about how this whole nonsense about some pandemic was a Conservative plot to take over America.

CHAPTER TWO

PANDEMIC

15 MARCH 2118
MOUNDSVILLE, WV

The morning of 15 March brought chaos and the predicted worldwide pandemic. The entire world came under the spell of this devil virus between 15 and 16 March. No Hospitals were open as the medical staffs were also ill and therefore unable to assist other sufferers.

On 13 March 2118, not one of Jake's students had become ill. The Dig Team began to relax, thinking that maybe there would be no pandemic after all. That faint hope crashed back to reality during the night of 15 March when, as though an alarm went off, every member of the Dig Team began sneezing; by morning, there was only one person able to get out of bed. Gale Storm had a bit of sniffling and sneezing, but beyond that, she felt okay. It was because of this small miracle that Jake survived when so many others died.

Gale tried to keep her team hydrated and fed. She helped them to the Porta-Potties, but still a bit over half of them died.

On day seven of the pandemic, Gale was nearly frantic as it appeared that Jake was teetering over the abyss of death. She cried and prayed as she kept cool, damp rags on his forehead and force-fed her love with broth.

Each day Death made the rounds of the University Dig Team, but Jake began to slowly back away from the Grim Reaper's Scythe.

For ten days everything across the world closed down as there were none strong enough to even leave their homes. Billions died from the flu, starvation, and dehydration. Millions more died from diseases such as dysentery, lack of insulin, failed medical devices, and a myriad of other reasons.

In ten days, the human population of the entire Earth fell to less than two-billion survivors.

25 MARCH 2118, 0700
HEADQUARTERS, 175TH RANGER REGIMENT,
FORT BENNING, GA

Colonel Tom Merritt, the 175th Ranger, Regimental Commander, awoke feeling like he might survive this horrible flu, that had swept the world, after all. The last ten days had nearly convinced him, on several occasions, that he would not live through this pandemic.

Tom was a confirmed bachelor who, as a young man, dedicated his life and love to the Army of the United States of America. While Tom didn't have movie star looks, he stood 5'11 with sandy blonde hair, coupled with an athletic build. His face was average and friendly, well, except for the faint scar that ran down his right cheek. You had to look closely to even see it clearly, but somehow it did make his facial features seem just a tiny bit out of kilter. Still, even with some minor defects, it had been those blue eyes that set many a young heart to flutter. Now, after twenty years of hard service as an Army Ranger, his body remained fit and athletic. His face had acquired many more wrinkles than his forty-two years should have held, and those eyes of boyish blue had evolved into Arctic blue ice. After two decades of service to his country, Tom Merritt had matured into a no-nonsense professional soldier.

He decided that reporting in to the Fort Benning Post Commander would be the proper course of action before going to his Headquarters. At this point in time, Colonel Tom Merritt had no inkling of the devastating impact this pandemic had caused the world at large. He turned on his radio but heard only a Conelrad station reminding everyone to remain calm.

By 0900 hours Tom felt better than he had in a long time, and he seemed to be getting better by the hour. Upon leaving his Quarters, his nostrils were immediately assaulted with the sickly-sweet stench of death. The realization that the toll of the dead must be huge, coupled with the penetrating smell caused him to reel back into the house. Quickly closing the door, he made his way to his garage and found several painter's masks. Tom coated one of the masks with some of his aftershave before placing it over his nose and mouth.

He again left his home and made his way to the 2116 Ford Aero-car. He backed his car onto the street and lifted into the air to an altitude of two hundred feet and keeping his craft between the lane marking buoys headed off to Fort Benning. The virtual lane markers appeared on the windshield in 3-D relief as soon as the driver entered a destination. Onboard computers kept the Aero-Car within the safe boundaries along his route.

Colonel Merritt's FooF (Friend or Foe) beacon identified and cleared him onto Fort Benning. As he made his way to the Post Headquarters Building, Tom searched, but could see no other vehicles either in the air or on the ground.

Now he was becoming worried; the parking lot fronting the Fort Benning Headquarters sat empty. There was no one walking around. The Fort appeared deserted. No, wait, there's a ground car pulling into the parking lot.

The Colonel's AI took control of the vehicle and sat his Aero-car down smoothly. He then pulled into a parking space near the other new arrival. As he exited his vehicle, an E-6 Staff Sergeant walked up to Tom and saluted.

Looking at Tom's nametag, the Sergeant said, "Colonel, uh, Merritt, sir, it is so good to see you. Do you know how bad things are?"

Merritt returned the salute and checking the Sergeant's nametag, asked, "No, Sergeant Evans, have you seen anyone else?"

"Yes, sir, I did see two other vehicles on Post. Hopefully, they'll come here with some info."

"I do hope so," said Merritt, "come with me and let's take a look inside. Maybe the Staff Duty Officer or NCO is there." The two men walked side by side, with the Sergeant on the Colonel's left, up the steps to the Headquarters Building.

The main door was unlocked, which gave both men some encouragement, but once inside they found the building completely unattended. Dust had already begun to settle everywhere.

"Oh, crap, sir, what should we do?"

"Sergeant, do you work in this building?"

"Yes, sir, I work in the 18th Airborne Corps, Command Communications Section. It's on the third floor of this building."

"Well, there's a break. All right, lead the way to communications and let's see if we can contact Mount Weather. They should have some idea of what the hell is going on."

Just as Merritt and Evans turned to move to the communications room, the outer door opened, and two young men entered. Both men were E-5 Buck Sergeants, Jack Price and Jaime "Moe" Morales

The two newcomers were very happy to see Colonel Merritt and Sergeant Evans. They both reported to Colonel Merritt before asking the now, usual questions.

"All right, hold on, let's begin by learning a bit about each other. My name is Colonel Tom Merritt, Commanding the 175th Ranger Regiment. Sergeant Evans?"

"Yes, sir, I'm Staff Sergeant Jim Evans, Commo Section, 18th Airborne Corps." He then pointed to Sergeant Price."

"Yes, sir, I'm Sergeant Jack Price, Assistant Squad Leader, Bravo Company, 75th Ranger Battalion."

Sergeant Morales spoke up saying, "Sir, I am Sergeant Jaime Morales, but everyone calls me Moe. I am the Armorer for Bravo Company, 75th Ranger Battalion."

Tom then asked, "How is everyone feeling? Are you fully recovered?"

Both Staff Sergeant Evans and Sergeant Morales said they felt good and ready for duty. Sergeant Price said that he felt okay, but still just a little weak.

"Well, all right," said Colonel Merritt, "it looks like we have the cadre of an army to build on. Sergeant Evans, please lead on to Commo."

Staff Sergeant Evans then turned to lead the four men to the 3rd-floor Communication's Room. Like every other office they passed, it was empty.

Evans turned on the office lights and made his way to his station. "Sir, from here, you can either hold this device over your AI chip to download the entire military communications network in CONUS (Continental U.S.). Or, I can make contact with Mount Weather for you."

"Thank you, Sergeant Evans, I think I would like to have both. Let's download to my AI, then place a speaker call to Mount Weather. Lori, you with us?"

Tom, darling, you know full well that I am always here for you, said Lori, Tom's soothing and sometimes flirtatious female-voiced AI.

Six years ago, when he reached the rank of Lieutenant Colonel, Tom was required to accept an Artificial Intelligence chip or retire. His AI could be either male or female.

Tom couldn't readily explain why he had chosen a female AI, but over the few years since they were mated, it just seemed to work. Her capabilities and duties were exactly the same as the male counterparts. Lori was strictly professional when the circumstances required but could be cute and funny at other times. Tom discovered that Lori made for a warm and comforting companion especially when he was feeling a bit deflated. She could also be somewhat snarky at times. All military AIs had this snarkyness built into their programming to help keep the owner more alert and on his or her toes. This feature could also be temporarily turned off with a simple command.

Placing the hand-held device over the left hemisphere of his brain, Tom downloaded the network communications data to Lori, then directed Evans to place the call.

There was initially a delayed response from Mount Weather Operations. When they finally answered, Colonel Merritt identified himself and was connected to General Howard.

"Colonel Merritt, it is good to hear that you made it through this horrible pandemic. How are things shaping up at Fort Benning?"

"Sir, currently I have found three others who have reported for duty, one Staff Sergeant, and two Buck Sergeants. The Staff Sergeant is assigned to 18th Airborne Corps communications. The two E-5s are both from Bravo Company of my Regiment, the 175th Rangers.

"No one else has, as yet, reported in, but I believe that there will be many others. The four of us currently present for duty just recovered this morning, and to our surprise, three of us feel better than we have in years; very strange, sir."

"Yes, that is most peculiar, I'll see that your recovery status is passed on to the CDC. Colonel, I surely hope that you are correct about survivors."

"Yes, sir, as do I."

"Good, good, Tom you had better keep an eye on the Sergeant who is not fully up to snuff, though. We wouldn't want a relapse. Once around the block with this Super-flu is more than enough for anyone. Now, what is your plan for today?"

"Yes, sir, I plan to commandeer Staff Sergeant Evans and return to my Regimental HQ. I am hopeful that I will find more Rangers reporting in for duty. I also intend to send one of the E-5s on a scouting mission to get a count of available rations. Once we have a few more, I will begin securing rations, Class V (Munitions), fuel, and our water supply."

"Very well," said General Howard, "I like your plan. Colonel, I am going out on a limb here in telling you what, we believe, is coming. On 7 March we suffered a breach of the main door when the Duty Officer decided to bring in civilians who were outside begging to be let in. He shot the guard and opened the door. Five children made it inside before the door could be secured. That three or four-minute opening allowed the virus to get into the Mount Weather Facility. We all fell ill. We're just beginning to discover who, and how many made it. The death toll is staggering."

"Yes, sir," said Colonel Merritt, "the air is carrying the sickly-sweet smell of rotting human flesh. Everyone is constantly near to, and often are, vomiting. I have sent two of my new force to find painter's masks. Perhaps that will help."

"Good thinking, Tom, now, comes the worst part; you must, at once, begin arming all survivors, because the worst is yet to come. In four days, roughly half of the survivors worldwide will go into hiding. Four days after that you will be at war with Cavemen. I know, I know, it sounds crazy, but this has already happened on board the three mining ships which altered the orbit of Holly Thorne. Don't worry about the Mags being armed. They will not have a clue what firearms are, or how to use any weapon other than clubs."

"Roger, sir," said Tom, who was almost in a state of shock."

General Howard continued, "Those who go into hiding will morph, devolve, whatever the hell you want to call it, into Cro-Magnon men. They are our closest cousins along the evolutionary line. If you come across any of these hiders, we call them Mags, you must kill them at once. Tom, there can be no exceptions. Kill 'em! Every single one you find. Who they were no longer matters. They were once human but will have devolved into the Cro-Magnon Man. They seem to instinctively have the need to wipe out all who they think may be competition. That is something we cannot allow.

"One thing is for certain; the civilian population is going to take an early beating. When they come out of hiding, they will attack anyone who is not a Mag. Am I absolutely clear on this, Colonel?"

"Yes, sir, of course, but that is a lot to process. I'll begin arming our people this morning, but to be completely honest, you have just scared the living crap out of me. I mean, sir, I could become one of these Mags."

"I'm sorry, Tom, but you are right, we all might. Data from the Mining Ships indicates that survivors have a 50% chance of turning. I pray you are not one of them."

The Colonel managed an ironic smile and said, "Well, General, that makes two prayers for me; yours and mine."

Tom added, "Sir, how about we schedule update contacts at 0800 and 1700 daily?"

"Good plan, Tom. I have one more item to discuss with you. My friend, if our facility is destroyed, you must contact the Cheyenne Mountain Facility. It has not been compromised, and so it is still functioning. The VPOTUS is there. I will pass info about our discussion to General Hank Morse. I'm sure he will be my replacement, should the worst happen. Tom, I have a meeting with the President, so I've got to run. I'll fill her in on your humble beginnings. Out, here."

And with that, Colonel Tom Merritt had his marching orders; arm the troops and draft everyone who makes it back to Benning into some modicum of a functioning military force.

25 MARCH 2118
MOUNT PALOMAR OBSERVATORY
CALIFORNIA

Trent Allison awoke and felt better, much better. For the first time in days, he was able to shower, brush his teeth, and not experience jet-propelled diarrhea. In fact, he realized that he was literally feeling stronger by the moment. He had kept an audio journal beginning with the onset of the Super-flu.

Journal entry for 25 March 2118, I have survived and am not only over the flu, but I can't remember when I have felt better, although a meal wouldn't hurt my feelings any.

As an afterthought, Trent added another note: *I shouldn't have named that damned Comet, Holly Thorne. That stupid ex of mine even ruined the greatest light show in history.*

28 MARCH 2118, 0800
175TH RANGER REGIMENTAL HQ
FORT BENNING, GA

By 28 March, Colonel Merritt's force stood at well over ten thousand men and women. While this seemed a large number, Tom's force amounted to less than 5% of the pre-flu active military personnel stationed at Fort Benning. To make matters even worse, the Officer Corps stood at only 10% of assigned strength. The highest ranking surviving officers reporting to Colonel Merritt were twenty-five Lt Colonels.

The NCO Corps was also hard hit, as the most senior NCOs were E-7 Platoon Sergeants. Officers and NCOs were, therefore, placed in positions well above their pay-grade. Merritt had decided to wait on promotions until he was sure the last of the stragglers reported for duty.

Colonel Merritt directed the Chain of Command to get the names and rank, along with any noteworthy after effects of the Super-flu. This survey provided both a complete roster of available personnel and how they had felt since their recovery.

The report that arrived on Tom's desk showed that roughly 50% of the survivors felt great, while the other half were somewhat tired and not quite up to par. He forwarded this info up the chain to the CDC.

Four days later, on 29 March 2118, nearly one-billion survivors, around the world, went into hiding. Roughly five-thousand in Colonel Tom Merritt's command disappeared.

25 MARCH 2118
TRENT ALLISON'S HOME
TEMECULA, CALIFORNIA

Trent spent the first morning of his recovery in an orgy of feasting. He ate until his stomach screamed for him to give it a break. In retaliation, his gut decided to make him pay for the overindulgent feeding frenzy. The first pains of bloating and abdominal pressure began about twenty minutes following his meal. The toilet beckoned and would not be put off.

When Trent decided to get dressed to make his way into the world to discover the results of the Super-Flu, he discovered that all of his clothes were way too large. In wonderment, he stood straight and looked down. "Holy crap," shouted Trent, "I can see my feet, and, oh my God, I can even see my belt buckle." This revelation made him realize that he would have to go and buy some new duds.

Trent suddenly realized that he had not put his glasses on, but he could see fine. He picked up the glasses from his bedside and placed them on his face. He simply could not believe that with his glasses on the world was a blur; without them, he could see perfectly. Trent couldn't stop grinning.

The day was spectacular with only a light breeze, bright sunshine, and temperatures in the low to mid-seventies. "Damn, what a gorgeous day," shouted Trent Allison to the skies above.

Taking a deep breath, Trent nearly fell to the ground from a sickly-sweet smell. It was somewhat like the odor he would expect from rotting pork. The breeze from the Pacific Ocean had somewhat filtered the smell, but what there was sent him reeling from nausea.

He made his way to his one extravagance, a fusion-powered Musk pickup and quickly turned up the air-conditioning, which helped diminish the rotten pork smell. He began driving to the nearest Walmart Supercenter at 32225 Temecula Pkwy. As he drove along, he was surprised to see that very few people were out and about. Trent considered the possibility that most were still ill, or the Super-flu had proved to be much deadlier than he had believed possible. He turned on the truck radio and heard only static until he came upon a Conelrad station, which was playing a continuous loop. The loop was the same one that had been playing the day before the flu struck. Oh, crap, thought Trent, that cannot be good.

The parking lot at the Supercenter held only five other cars, all parked near the entrance.

As Trent was about to get out of his short bed pickup, he tied a handkerchief over his nose. It was then he had a nagging thought that rapidly made its way to the surface of his conscious mind. End of the world, good guys, bad guys. He was happy for the national right to carry law, passed some eighty years earlier. He reached under his seat and removed a small 9mm pistol in a waistband holster.

Before Trent had become ill, he was a pudgy, early middle-aged man of forty. He stood 5' 7" tall, with male pattern baldness. His profession as an astronomer caused his skin to have a pale sheen that bordered on porcelain. He wore glasses, had a small chin, large nose, and was known to be a sloppy dresser.

As Trent began to make his way to the entrance, he ran his hand over his head and stopped dead in his tracks. He again slowly ran his hand over the top of his head; fuzz, a fine fuzz was growing on his previously bald pate. Again, he rubbed and rubbed to prove to himself that he truly had hair growing where he had been bald since his early twenties. This discovery added a bit of pep to his step and placed a big smile on his face.

Trent approached the door and saw that it had been forced open. The inside was not quite dark, but more like the final fading light of dusk. Initially, he thought that perhaps he should leave and try to do his shopping somewhere more inviting. He began to turn around when a voice said, "Don't worry, it's okay, come on in."

Trent turned to run back to his car when a man in a Policeman's uniform stepped from the shadows. Seeing that the voice had been that of a Cop caused Trent to become a little more relaxed.

The Officer smiled at Trent and said, "It's okay, there are a few people inside doing some shopping. At first, I thought I should run them off, then decided that in this emergency I'd just ask anyone coming in to leave their name and phone number by the registers. Hell, I doubt if anyone will ever call them, but it just seemed like the right thing to do."

Trent looked at the man's nametag which read, Jones. He said, "Officer Jones, do you have any idea of the magnitude of this pandemic?"

Jones looked sad as he said, "Not really, but my guess comes from the number of Officers reporting for duty. Out of one-hundred and twenty, twenty-eight have reported in. If that is an indicator, then the death toll here in Temecula will be near one-hundred thousand. Ten days ago, the population was near one-hundred and forty-thousand."

"Oh, dear God," said a shaken Trent Allison, "is that even possible?"

"Yeah, it is. I spent most of the morning entering the homes of our brother officers. I found no one alive, and the smell of death was overpowering."

After a few seconds, Officer Jones regained his composure and said, "Let's change the subject for a bit. I see that you've lost some weight and I'll bet you could use some clothes that fit, so come on in and take what you need. With so many dead, those of us still around have got to help each other, you know?"

At just that moment a solemn young woman pushing a cart emerged from the store and after thanking the officer went to her car. This small thing made Trent feel much more at ease, and he decided to go ahead in to get some clothes that fit.

His eyes slowly adjusted to the low light and he saw a few others pushing carts around the store. Trent quickly found a couple of outfits that fit, then searched the home goods section and found the seal-a-meal machine. Almost as an afterthought, he decided to stock up on some canned goods before making his way back to the exit.

Trent intended to thank the Policeman, but when he arrived at the door, Officer Jones was no longer there; still, his presence had made an impression on Trent. The country may be trashed, but good people are still around.

Yes, good people were still around, but many, like Officer Jones, were in shock and just going through the motions…

CHAPTER THREE

THE TURNING

25 MARCH 2118
COMMUNICATIONS ROOM
CHEYENNE MOUNTAIN

Admiral Huxley entered the Communications Room at the Cheyenne Mountain Facility. The senior Naval Officer on Duty shouted, "Admiral on deck!" which caused everyone to jump to attention.

"Carry on, as you were," ordered Huxley, as an Air Force Captain approached and offered his hand to the Admiral.

"Good morning, Admiral, is there something you need?"

"Yes, please put me in contact with Admiral Perry aboard the Wake Island," said Huxley.

"Yes, sir, of course. Sir," said the Duty Officer, "would you like a cup of coffee while the satellite routes the call. It will take approximately five minutes for the signal to reach the Wake Island."

"Thank you, Captain, that would be fine."

Some five minutes later the Space Fleet, *en route* to the Red Sands Colony on Mars came on the line. The irrepressible Admiral Perry said, "Hux, how they hangin' old son?"

Admiral Huxley, a more old school Naval Flag Officer, was a bit miffed when he replied, "Really, Admiral, show some decorum on an open line."

"Sure, Hux, you old stuffed shirt, okay, okay, I apologize. Admiral Huxley, what traffic do you have for me?"

Huxley was a bit exasperated at his Academy Classmate, but he could not completely hide the trace of a smile. Everyone else in the Communications Center was trying to pretend not to have heard the exchange between the two Admirals. The ten-minute delay only made the entire scene appear more frustratingly comedic.

Abruptly, Huxley ordered the Duty Officer to inform Admiral Perry that he would send a sub-space communique outlining the events at Cheyenne Mountain.

25 MARCH 2118
USSDF WAKE ISLAND
CONVOY TRAVELING TO MARS COLONY

Onboard the USSDF Cruiser, Wake Island, both Admiral Adolphus Perry and "Sky" King chuckled at Huxley's apparent discomfort. "That old sod never could take a joke, but stuffed shirt or not, I like that old fart. Sky, you'd better put together a report on our progress to Red Sands."

Still smiling, Admiral Sky King said, "Sure, Dolf, I'll have it to you in a couple of hours."

25 MARCH 2118
SOUTH COAST WINERY RESORT
TEMECULA, CALIFORNIA

As Trent left the Walmart parking lot, he aimed his car toward the Home Depot when he realized that there was really no real reason to return to his modest, one-bedroom cottage. He called it his hovel.

Trent decided to visit one of his favorite Sunday afternoon haunts, probably his one-real extravagance, the South Coast Winery Resort. There were many pleasant memories for a solitary figure like Trent. The winery grounds provided magnificent views of the vineyard and the surrounding vistas. He loved to sit with a bottle of wine and a wedge of cheese on the warm, shaded verandas while enjoying a book by Cliff Deane, as the gentle trade winds blew across his body from the Pacific Ocean.

Though Trent had been to the Winery many times, he didn't feel he could afford to stay in one of the Resort rooms. As he drove along, he said, "What the hell, if the place is deserted, then I may as well have some wine and enjoy the best suite in the house for a couple of days, until I figure out what to do next. Yeah, why go home and live like a peasant, when I can go just about anywhere and live like a King, at least for a while."

Being alone had never been a concern to Trent as he spent nearly all of his time at the Observatory in quiet solitude.

It took only a few minutes to arrive at the Home Depot. Again, the parking lot was empty, so he parked across the front entrance and kicked in the glass door. Once inside he went straight to the painting masks to use as replacements for his handkerchief before finding the generators. Trent managed to wrestle a 5.5 KwH Fusion Ryobi model into the back of his pickup. Returning to the store, he found a small propane grill and several small cans of propane. He felt stronger than he ever had, healthier, too and he liked it.

Almost as an afterthought, he grabbed a set of grilling tools. He now felt ready to enjoy a few days of pleasant tranquility, back at the Winery.

Trent thought, just one more stop, and I'll be all set. He set a course for the Temecula Public Library. Once inside he began selecting a few books to read for pleasure on the Veranda, before beginning his primary task of selecting survival books. First on his list were the Foxfire books. After two hours of scouring the library he came to the last on his list; How Things Work. As he looked at the two large stacks of books, he realized that the finding was easier than the carrying would be.

25 APRIL 2118
HOTEL ST. MICHAEL
GURLEY ST,
PRESCOTT, ARIZONA

Colonel Cindy Sharp retired from the Army in August of 2117. She had spent nearly all of her twenty-five years of service in foreign countries. Her military resume told the story of a Cobra Gunship Pilot that had served eight distinguished combat tours of duty; all of which she had volunteered. Her many awards centered around two Silver Stars for valor, and two Purple Hearts.

Cindy was twenty-two when she took the Soldiers Oath upon graduation from West Point, where she graduated at the top of the class of 2092. The next step in her journey took her to Flight School, where she so excelled in the operation of rotary winged aircraft that she graduated first in her class. She immediately submitted a request for combat air training.

As Sharp's experience grew, she was rapidly promoted through, what the Army called "First Look." This program allowed the top three percent of Officers to be considered for promotion one year ahead of their peers in the normal course of career progression.

Colonel Cindy Sharp was a handsome woman but was committed to her career and did not marry.

She was on the fast track to General's Stars, but, unfortunately for the U.S. Army, Colonel Sharp had no desire to become a General. What she did desire was to spend the first year of her retirement traveling the forty-eight contiguous United States, in search of a home before she became too, in her mind, old. She planned to spend a minimum of a week in each, before settling into retirement.

Her arrival in Prescott came just a week before the Earth's passage through the tail of the Holly Thorne Comet. The following four days were spent visiting the historical sites around Prescott, the original Territorial Capital of Arizona. The Grand Canyon evoked a deep yearning to learn more about this incredible feature. She also especially enjoyed the Phippen Museum, with its amazing Western Art collection.

Cindy's evenings were spent around Whiskey Row's historic saloons, and, of course, the regularly scheduled events just across the street on the lawn of the Courthouse.

While Cindy enjoyed the culinary delights of Prescott, she became especially enamored with the oldest saloon and restaurant in Arizona, the Palace Saloon. Doc Holliday and his companion, Big Nose Kate spent quite a bit of time playing poker there. Actually, the Palace Saloon burned down two times in its history, but each time the bar's patrons lifted the bar and carried it across the street to keep it from burning.

For the last one-hundred years, the saloon became more oriented toward being a first-rate restaurant and saloon. The gambling and brothel were gone, but their history lived on via the photos and gambling equipment on display. Local Cowboys, dressed in period clothing still wandered in for a beer or two, adding to the Old West ambiance.

In 1972 the Palace had a prominent role in the hit movie, *Junior Bonner* starring Steve McQueen, Ida Lupino, and Robert Preston. The film centered around McQueen as a Rodeo Man.

Cindy Sharp, like so many others who come to Prescott, fell in love with the surrounding area of the Prescott Basin. She knew right away that this would be her retirement home. Her plan was to buy a home in Williamson Valley, but, like the rest of the world, Cindy became ill with the Super-Flu. Before becoming sick, she managed to stock her Hotel Room in the St. Michael with the supplies recommended by President Holcomb.

Her sickness lasted the typical ten days, eight of which she wanted to die. On day ten, Cindy began to improve and soon felt wonderful. She ate a Clif's Bar, showered, dressed, and, as always strapped her sidearm onto her belt in the cross-draw position of eighteen degrees.

Cindy believed in taking the world as it came and dealing with each new situation just as it presented itself. She also knew that she was unlikely to win a fight with a large, strong man. Running away was not in her nature, so she was thankful that Mr. Colt had leveled the playing field. She regularly practiced her quick draw, along with accuracy training to further enhance her chances of survival in a fight, and though she also carried a surgically sharp knife sheathed at the top of her spine, she was not one to bring only a knife to a gunfight.

Colonel Sharp spent the next four days volunteering with the Prescott and Tribal Police to assist in organizing a cleanup of bodies. This task was such a huge undertaking it quickly became obvious that the process would take more than a year.

With a population of around sixty-thousand, Prescott's dead was estimated to be around forty-five thousand. That left only fifteen-thousand available to get the town back up and running.

While, on the surface, that number seemed adequate for the job, in reality, it was impossible as far too many of those leaders needed to organize this task were dead. The Social, Medical, Engineering and Police forces had become leaderless. This added a huge power vacuum that would take time to fill.

As much of the community was in such a deep state of mourning from the loss of family and friends very little was able to be accomplished.

Then, on the morning of 29 March Cindy reported for volunteer duty, she discovered that nearly one-half of the population had disappeared.

28 MARCH 2118, 0800
175TH RANGER REGIMENTAL HQ
FORT BENNING, GA

On the morning of 28 March, Colonel Merritt had ordered that his command take up a bivouac, of sorts, in the Fort Benning Airport for a minimum of five days. On 29 March 2118, nearly one-billion survivors, around the world, went into hiding.

As he had been warned, on 29 March, Colonel Merritt discovered that nearly half of his command was absent from Company roll calls. His Officer and NCO Cadres were also cut in half. Roughly five-thousand of Colonel Tom Merritt's command disappeared or tried to.

Tom directed the Sergeant Major to spot check the list of hiders against the list of those who had not felt completely recovered. He discovered that nearly all of those who did not feel really good and strong had gone into hiding. He was saddened to see the name of Sergeant Price on the list of the missing.

The Colonel ordered the remaining troops to gather in a nearby hanger, where he explained what had happened and what must be done.

"Soldiers of the Army of the United States of America, what I have to order you to do will be the most difficult assignment of your lives. As you now know, last night we experienced what could be called a desertion rate of around 50%. Actually, I wish that desertion was the case, sadly it is not. During the night, roughly half of our force went into hiding. They are somewhere in the confines of the airport terminal, and we must find each and every one of them."

Tom hesitated before continuing, "No, the word hiding may not be accurate, but it is the only word I can think of to explain their absence. They are not hiding from their duty. They are hiding because that damned Super-flu caused by the Holly Thorne comet has inflicted another dire sucker punch right on our chin.

"This morning I spoke with General Howard at the Mount Weather Facility. He informed me that half of his Super-flu survivors, both military and civilian, have also gone into hiding.

"He additionally informed me that the senior staff at the Mount Weather Bunker expected this to happen. I was told that the three Mining Vessels tasked with moving that damned comet suffered the same fate.

"All right, what I am going to tell you next will require a lot of self-control, so I need everyone to Soldier-Up because here comes the sucker punch. Oooh-Rah?"

The response among these soldiers was tepid at best as the responding Oooh-Rah was almost whispered. Colonel Merritt then shouted, "OOH-RAH!" The response was better, but far from Merritt's Ranger roots. Merritt again shouted, "I SAID, OOH-RAH!"

Professionalism and Esprit de Corps finally kicked in, and the responding OOH-RAH became deafening.

"Well," said, the Colonel, "that's more like it. You are American Soldiers, I'm glad to hear that you remember who and what you are; warriors! You are the last hope for America. We will never falter or shy away from our duty to preserve this nation and the citizens of this great country."

The tension in the Hanger instantly became intense as the soldiers who had just survived the worst disaster in human history now faced yet another sharp stick in the eye. These were men and women of the United States Army who had just lost husbands, wives, children, parents, siblings, relatives, and friends. Their lives now had only one adhesive, their comrades in arms. For most, their loss had been so severe that only this bond could stave off insanity.

Because so many of the sick had opened the windows of their homes to air them out, the air now stank of rotting flesh, what else could possibly happen that could be as bad, or worse than what these men and women had already suffered? Zombies?

Every soldier there knew that their leader, Colonel Merritt, was a great man and would expect nothing less than dedication and excellence from each man and woman present. Their spirits began to soar which caused their heads to come back up as their spines began to stiffen.

'Go ahead, hit me with your best shot', became the mantra from this group of dedicated Americans. The phrase, hit me with your best shot, began as a single shout, then another, and another until, within seconds every voice was screaming the new term which would define this force; hit me with your best shot!

Merritt allowed the shouting to continue for another moment before raising his hand for silence. His face exuded confidence and portrayed a broad smile.

When the Hanger again became quiet, Colonel Merritt said, "I have spent more than two decades in this man's army, leading the finest Special Troopers in the world, but I must say that I have never been more proud of anyone, than I am of you. You have stiffened my backbone to match your own. Now I know without any consideration of failure that WE WILL SUCCESSFULLY DEFEND THIS NATION, AGAINST ANY ENEMY! OOH-RAH!"

The Hanger erupted with shouts of defiance to any threat. Whatever was to come would not defeat Merritt's Marauders. Again, their leader raised his hand for silence.

"All right, here it is. Those who have gone into hiding have begun devolving into one of Man's ancestors, the Cro-Magnon. These were cavemen who destroyed the Neanderthals, who had lived along the glacier's edge of the last Ice Age for one-hundred thousand years. If the hiders are left alone, in four days, they will return to us as Cro-Magnons. They will come out fighting. We must not let this happen.

"I have brought you here, to this airport, because the places to hide are somewhat limited. I know, I know, there must be a million places to hide here, but, at least they are not spread all over Fort Benning."

At this point, the projection screen displayed the video of the battle at the Mount Weather Bunker. Those present watched in stunned silence as the battle unfolded. The President, her Chief of Staff, both became hiders. Once they emerged, they were unrecognizable and were buried in the mass grave of Mags.

The news did indeed feel like a sucker punch to the gut, but now they knew what they would face.

Oh, crap, thought most of the soldiers in the Hanger, *no, these are not Zombies, they are far worse. Well, this is my country, and no monsters are going to take it away from me.*

The first Mag hunt had begun.

30 MARCH 2118, 0700
NATIONAL GUARD ARMORY
MOUNDSVILLE, WV

The WVU dig team, led by Professor Jacob Abraham, and his Assistant, Gale Storm had begun warily searching for any members of the team who had gone missing. They worked their way through the National Guard Armory in search of newly turned Mags. The Conelrad station had begun a repeating loop explaining why so many people had gone into hiding. The radio made it clear that all survivors were to arm themselves and prepare for an attack by Cavemen. This loop explained what was happening to those who were now missing.

The Armory search found only two hiders, who were now on the first day of their transformation. Even though Jake knew that he must kill these abominations, his intellectual side, coupled with his desire to record this incredible transformation, made him hesitate. He felt no particular qualm about destroying what he saw, but he felt that it might be important to follow the devolution of these sad creatures. Both of what the Professor now referred to as specimens were readily identified by sex, hair color, and dress. They had been Dave and Donna.

Jacob placed guards to watch over the specimen mutants. The guards maintained a continuous, 24/7 documentary. They also made notes further describing what occurred while they were on their two-hour shifts. Professor Abraham made his rounds every two hours making additional notes and taking photos of the progression of this terrifying metamorphosis into the Cro-Magnon Caveman.

Jake regretted not locking the exit doors from the Armory. He felt sure that the other four missing persons had made their way to a more secure setting. At around 2:00 pm Jake heard a scratching sound. It seemed to be coming from the side door leading into the building.

Jake alerted Gale, and they made their way carefully to the door. There were windows in the top half of the door, but the scratching sound was coming from the exit's lower third.

Both Jake and Gale were frightened, yet, they knew it was important to discover, who, or what, was trying to gain entrance into the Armory.

They crept in a very low crouch to keep from being visible to anyone on the outside. Jake whispered to Gale to remain hidden and ready for trouble. Jake slowly began to rise to a position which might allow him to see who was on the other side of the door.

Just as Jake's face rose high enough to be able to see the intruder, another face, a non-human face, appeared at the same instant. Jake screamed, "NO!" and was so startled that he fell painfully onto his tailbone. Gale also screamed in surprise. At first, he wondered why Gale didn't fire, then when she began to laugh, he realized the face that had so frightened them was a beautiful Chocolate Lab that wanted inside.

Now, Jake looked carefully in all directions before opening the door to allow the poor dog entrance. As soon as the door was barely open enough for the dog to squeeze through, he bounded into the hallway and began jumping and licking Jake. The poor animal was very thin and obviously starved for human company. It actually took several minutes for the Lab to calm down as he went back and forth between Jake and Gale.

Hunger and exhaustion finally brought the dog to settle down with his leg and right paw on Jake's lap. The dog's eyes were glistening with happiness as he looked up at Jake.

Gale continued to laugh and finally said, "Jake, it looks like you have a new friend. Come on, let's get him something to eat."

In the Gym, which also served as the Mess Hall, Gale found some cans of spam. Jake had been inspecting the dog and found a small collar which had a metal tag that read, Sergeant. Russell, K-9, Moundsville PD.

As Russell was making short work of the spam, Jake said, "Russell, come." The dog immediately stopped eating and rushed to Jake seeking attention and approval. After scratching his dog's ears and telling him what a good boy he was, Jake said, "Okay, Russ, go and eat." Russell then rushed back to his spam with tail wagging.

Gale had watched and said, "Well, dang, you've got a dog that is obviously smarter than either of us."

Jake just smiled before saying, "So it would appear. I think I'll keep him."

Gale again broke out laughing, "Really, Sherlock? My guess is that you don't have any say in the matter. You have just become Russell's human."

Jake began to chuckle and said, "Yeppers, that is the bare-naked truth."

2 APRIL 2118, 0800
CDC
SECURE LEVEL 5 LABS BUILDING
1600 CLIFTON RD NE, ATLANTA, GA 30329

The First Platoon of Company A, 2-5 Marine Battalion under the command of Lieutenant Geraldo Perez, out of Camp Lejeune had been flown in to secure the CDC. Before their departure, the platoon had been restructured with only single men.

As Standard Operating Procedure (SOP), the Lieutenant and his Platoon Sergeant inspected their "Mag Trap." This trap had been built by the US Army Corps of Engineers when the Level 5 facilities had been restructured and expanded to house those who would be quartered for the duration of the disease, or until a vaccine could be found.

The trap was a simple open glass cubicle. When a Mag entered this space, the door would slam shut behind him, and the small enclosure which was also an elevator would descend five floors to a secured Level

5 Mag Cell. Once the Mag was locked in this small, glass-walled elevator, gas would be released causing the Mag to become unconscious.

From there, robotic machinery would remove the Mag and place him on a medical evaluation gurney. It would then be transported to a research lab. Once in the lab and secured, the Mag would be made available to the Medical Research Personnel who would begin running tests to find a cure or a vaccine.

3 APRIL 2118, 1300
NATIONAL GUARD ARMORY
MOUNDSVILLE, WV

Professor Jacob Abraham made meticulous notes regarding the progression of the physical transformation from human to Mag.

By 1:00 pm on the 2nd of April a metamorphosis was happening with ever-increasing speed. The video and team notes described the trip from Human to Mag as a journey through pain and brutal deformation. Initially, the Mag's skin began to sag dramatically. The body took on a sheen of sweat as it began to transform fatty tissues into muscle. It quickly became apparent why the Mags were so strong. A Human Being would have to have intense workouts over a period of months to attain the physique of a Mag.

Facial expressions of the unconscious creature displayed extreme pain as the skull began to soften and reshape itself into a slightly more squared condition. With all these changes happening so quickly, the pain must have been beyond intense.

However, it was the transformation of the eye sockets that seemed to make the unconscious Mag constantly wince from pain. Tears ran freely from all around the eye's orbital lobe.

Jake slowly reached down to touch the Mag's face to be able to provide a tactile note to his study. As he touched the cheek of what had once been his student, Dave, the eyes snapped open. At first, the expression was one of being startled but quickly turned to murderous rage.

Russel, Jake's dog, had been watching this procedure intently. When the Mag's face morphed from surprise to hostility, he growled and threw himself onto the Mag's chest and without hesitation ripped out his throat.

This act by Russell may have saved Jake from serious injury or possibly being killed, as the Mag, with amazing speed, grabbed Jake's shirt just as Russell landed on his chest. Blood gushed from the Mag's wound, covering both Russell and Jake, but quickly faded as he bled out and the heart stopped pumping. Jake shouted for Gale to get a specimen bottle used in excavations to secure a large sample of blood from the Mag.

Gale agreed and sent the guard for a bottle as she inspected Jake for injury or possible fluid intake from the Mag's blood. Fortunately, none of the blood had entered Jake's mouth, nose, or eyes, and having no wounds, it appeared that he would not have a problem with bodily fluid transmission. Gale then ordered both Jake and Russell into the shower, a very cold shower. Jake scrubbed both himself and Russell thoroughly to remove the last vestiges of Mag blood from their bodies.

As they exited the shower, Sarah took Russell to dry him off, but could not resist sneaking an approving glance at her naked Professor.

Jake spotted Sarah's peek and shouted, "Sarah, stop that, besides, the water was very cold."

Gale took charge of drying Jake's body while she made another inspection to ensure that he had no scratches that might have been open to the blood from Dave.

"Gale," said Jake, "destroy the other specimen. Do it now."

Gale looked up at Jake and said, "It's already done. No way I was going to take a chance of her awakening after seeing what happened with specimen one."

"Well done, Gale, well done."

4 APRIL 2118, 0550 HOURS
BIOMEYER HEALTH FITNESS CENTER
1525 CLIFTON RD NE FL 5, ATLANTA, GA 30322

Physical Therapist Warren Douglas became conscious at 0550 hours on 4 April 2118. He had no idea of how he had come to be in this strange enclosure. He felt compelled to find his family, but he first had to discover how to get out of this cave which seemed to have no apparent opening. As he lay in near total darkness upon the floor, Warren began looking warily around his prison, he noticed a faint light coming from under a barrier. Warren realized that this blockage must be removed to allow him to escape his confinement.

Strange, hazy memories flooded his mind. Images that he could not even begin to understand, and as in a dream, these memories and images began to rapidly fade from his conscious mind. Now, only the drive to find others of his kind mattered.

After making sure that he was not, at that exact moment, in any danger from Cave Bears, Warren crawled to the room door. He sniffed the dusty air wafting into this cave through the opening. Faint, but familiar odors of other clansmen greeted his nostrils. The realization that his prison denied him access to others of his clan brought forth a murderous fury as he finally placed his fingers under the door.

He began to jerk and pull at the door, which remained closed, with only a small movement. Warren, in anger and frustration, arose and backed away from the door before throwing his body, with a leading right shoulder, against this strange prison wall. He crashed into the door which withstood his onslaught. Again, he backed away, and on his second attempt, the door came flying open, causing the Mag to stumble and fall to the floor in the hallway.

Quickly rising to his feet, Warren looked at the door hanging limply by one hinge and grunted his victory. Being alone brought an uneasiness which drove him to begin searching for his clansmen. The gloom of almost total darkness of this strange cave made him feel vulnerable and weak. Guided only by his enhanced sense of smell, Warren moved through the maze-like confines of the building.

Warren came upon a room which held a small pool of water. His thirst drove him to drink, but upon tasting this water, he knew from the smell that it was not safe. He realized, without knowing why that he must not drink this water which was heavily chlorinated.

He roared his anger and frustration to the ceiling. His shouts, however, brought results as a few seconds later, he heard a call from one of his own kind. Warren, turning toward the sound, made his way through the darkness, toward that plaintive call for help.

It took only minutes for Warren to discover the source of that cry and placing his shoulder in the same way that led to his escape, he threw himself against the door. For his troubles, Warren received a painful shock to his shoulder as the door withstood his assault.

From inside the room, another Mag, Ken Park, threw himself against the door from the inside, and again, on the second attempt, it was torn from its hinges freeing him from his prison. Unfortunately, the door struck Warren, knocking him to the floor. He roared with pain and an ever-increasing anger.

Ken removed the door from Warren, then the two Mags began sniffing each other and finding the proper pheromones, joined forces to find their way into the light. The two men had worked together for two years, and that association led them to believe that they were from the same clan.

Together the two Mags eventually made their way toward the front entrance of the former medical rehab building.

The exit led into a heavy, wind-blown rain. The open air, however, was warm and comforting to these two Mags. Uncaringly, the two walked into the rain and reveled in the downpour which washed the wet, somewhat sticky slime from their bodies. Both Mags raised their heads and enjoyed their first drink of water in four days.

After being in near darkness, the daylight caused both Warren and Ken to squint momentarily until their vision became focused in the mid-morning light. This visual clarity brought fear as the immediate surroundings gave little in the way of opportunities for concealment.

Again, both Mags felt the disconcerting and hazy remnants of dream-like memories of these surroundings. On some level of fading consciousness, they knew that these strange caves held other creatures that were like, and yet unlike, themselves. Warren roared a challenge to those others who must be destroyed. Neither could fully understand the why of their need to kill the others. That deep seeded need rose from the primal, ancestral memory of available resources. After all, there were only so many Mammoths.

Their Mag nostrils were assaulted with smells that were incomprehensible; the two constants of these odors caused both anger and fear. Passing a small construction site, they found a long wooden 2X4. The strength of the Mag body made it easy to break the board into suitably long clubs. Seeking food and concealment, the two Mags began searching for their clan. This search took them in an easterly direction.

CHAPTER FOUR

4 APRIL 2118
MOUNT WEATHER

On 4 April 2118, the only survivors in Mount Weather were two Secret Service Officers and ninety-seven Rangers. The highest-ranking surviving member of the military was a Corporal.

In the final analysis, Second Lieutenant Dudley committed what he had hoped to prevent; the mass murder of thousands. Once exposed to this Mag-flu, survivors became immune from reinfection. Surprisingly, they seemed to also feel a renewed vigor and strength.

With thousands dead in Mount Weather, the Senior Secret Service Officer ordered the blast door opened for removal of the dead and burial.

Two members of the Comet Committee survived the flu, and both turned. President Greene and her Chief of Staff were unrecognizable. They would be buried along with the others in a mass grave.

4 APRIL 2118, 0900 HOURS
ST. MICHAEL HOTEL
GURLY ST., PRESCOTT, AZ

Cindy Sharpe turned on her battery-powered emergency radio in the hope of finding a Conelrad Station that might have some news. Near the mid-range of the FM Band, she found station KFNA broadcasting a news segment. She was stunned to hear a non-Conelrad station on the air.

"This is DJ Foote broadcasting on 99.9 FM. There are only two of us barricaded inside the station. Be alert, those survivors who disappeared four days ago have awakened, and they have turned into Cavemen. We just received notice from the CDC that these monsters are no longer Modern Humans. The Super-Flu has caused them to devolve into our nearest ancestor, Cro-Magnon Man. The Government calls them Mags.

"Please, everyone, arm yourselves. Reports are coming in of roving bands of Mags killing everyone they come across. NO! These are not Zombies, they are not the undead. These creatures are alive, fast, strong, and have only one thing on their mind; killing us. Please, do not hesitate, shoot first. If you don't act first, you will die.

"These things began to surface all over the world around dawn, local times. I am now going to broadcast the latest from the Cheyenne Mountain Facility."

A recording of both the American and World situation was then played two times before the station signed off until the top of the next hour.

I don't know how long we will be able to broadcast, but we will come back on the air at the top of each hour to bring you the latest, at least until we run out of diesel.

Around noon Cindy Sharp began hearing crashing sounds. Sounds that raised the hair on the back of her neck. The sounds were coming closer, and now she began hearing angry sounding grunts as doors were kicked in. She drew her pistol and waited patiently, albeit with no small amount of trepidation. The one thing she was sure of was that if anyone came through her door, that person would have to be carried out, dead.

She was in room 306. Room 307 was directly across the hall. The angry grunts became growling roars that sent images of wild beasts through Cindy's mind. She heard the door of 308 being kicked open, followed by a woman's scream. A terrified sound that was cut short and would never be finished.

"Well, screw this," said Cindy to the door just before it came crashing in. There, before her stood a creature holding a table leg. He should have been a figure in a wax museum of horrors. This monster saw Cindy Sharp standing her ground only eight feet away. His head cocked slightly to his right side as his face took on a puzzled look as though he was searching for some remote memory that refused to fully surface.

He found himself looking down the barrel of a pistol. His head again cocked slightly to the right side as he seemed to instinctively take on some faint understanding of danger. She said, "Smile, watch for the flash!" as she pulled the trigger two times. Both rounds hit the Mag in the heart, knocking him onto his back, dead well before he hit the ground.

In the enclosed environment of the room, the sharp, staccato sound of pistol fire was deafening as seventeen inches of flame shot out of the barrel. The familiar, strong odor of ozone filled the air which heightened Colonel Sharpe's senses.

Cindy made her way to the body of the Mag where she spent several moments studying this horror. The Mag was wearing touristy clothes, shorts, printed Tee, and sandals with black socks. The clothes were filthy and tainted with the rancid odor of urine and feces.

Stepping over the body Cindy cautiously investigated the darkened hallway, but there seemed to be no more of these disgusting things, at least not on her floor. Crossing the hallway, she entered Room 307 to see if the woman she heard scream could be helped. There on the floor lay the body of a middle-aged woman wearing an oversized house dress. No close inspection was needed as the woman's head was split open like a watermelon dropped onto the ground. The smell of death was heavy in this room, and Cindy understood why when she looked at the bed. There lay a man who had been dead for at least a week; killed by the Super-Flu.

She closed the broken door behind her and returned to her room. Cindy began searching her purse for the three additional fifteen round, 9 mm magazines loaded with hollow point ammunition. For just an instant she lamented the fact that her bug-out backpack was in the trunk of her car.

The one thing she was sure of was that she needed to get to her pack which held another two-hundred rounds of 9mm and a one-hundred-year-old Kel-Tec Sub-2000 folding carbine, chambered in 9 mil and using Glock magazines. The lightweight carbine was far from a long gun, but it was deadly out to around one-hundred yards with a very flat trajectory. At two hundred yards, the fall of the round is about six inches, requiring a bit of Kentucky windage, and Tennessee elevation.

Her friends had thought her weapons choices to be odd, and Cindy couldn't give any particular reason for her antiques other than she just liked twentieth-century firearms. "I carry what I like and take comfort in," was her usual response.

Before leaving the hotel, Cindy packed her belongings and took the bathroom hygiene products, then emptied the small fridge. Cindy didn't often drink alcohol, but she took those mini-bottles for trade or use as an antiseptic.

The hallway was dark, and the stink of rotting human flesh had begun to permeate the air. Cindy began breathing through her mouth as she took a small flashlight from her purse to light a path to the stairwell.

4 APRIL 2118
CHEYENNE MOUNTAIN
COLORADO SPRINGS, CO

"Sir," said Simon Ward, the Vice President's Chief of Staff, "we have just received word, along with a video feed of a Mag attack inside the Mount Weather Facility. The highest-ranking survivor is one, Leland Ball, a member of President Greene's Secret Service Detail. The highest ranking military person is a Corporal. Mr. Ball has assumed leadership of the survivors until an appropriate Military Command structure can be sent. He has opened Mount Weather to remove and bury the dead. Greene and her COS both turned. They were killed while attacking the surviving Rangers.

"It appears that I am the highest ranking civilian government official authorized to do the honor of swearing you in as President. The off-duty personnel here at Cheyenne Mountain are currently gathering in the theater to attend, and witness, your swearing in as the new President of the United States, whatever is left of it."

At 0945 hours, everyone with access to a radio heard the new U.S. President Vance Holcomb say, as he became the sixty-third President of the United States, "I do solemnly swear that I will faithfully execute the Office of President of the United States, and will, to the best of my Ability, preserve, protect, and defend the Constitution of the United States,"

Following the swearing-in ceremony now President Vance Holcomb was led to a conference room. There he was seated before a computer which replayed the battle between Mags and Man in the Mount Weather Facility.

He stared at the computer screen. His expression of horror left nothing to Simon's imagination. Holcomb was dumbfounded to the point of near shock. What he saw was violent and savage in the extreme. Just this morning he had learned about the death of President Eileen N. Greene, and his new task of destroying what General Morse called, that damned Mag infestation.

Before seeing the fierce conflict, President Holcomb had been hopeful that the Mags would still retain some semblance of humanity, he had held to the prospect that communication might be established between Mankind and these Mags; after all, they had been fellow human beings just a few days ago. After watching the Mount Weather video, President Holcomb understood that his hope now lay in tatters upon the floor, like the leaves of an elm tree rotting upon winter's frozen ground.

It took only a few moments to watch the footage from Mount Weather for President Holcomb to realize that General Morse had been absolutely correct in his description of the Mag infestation. This video was the introduction to Vance Holcomb's initial Presidential Briefing.

Around the table sat President Vance Holcomb, Lt. General Hank Morse, and Holcomb's Chief of Staff Simon Ward. The CDC, Fort Detrick, the Jet Propulsion Lab (JPL), the Palomar Observatory, and the Naval Academy were represented by holograms via satellite feeds.

These briefers brought the President up-to-speed on current events, both at home and around the world. The sporadic reports from around the country began to paint a grim picture, reminiscent of a painting of Hell by Hieronymus Bosch, as survivors from the varied governmental and military forces came back on-line. Across the board, the tale was identical; a worldwide collapse with a human population now numbering in the millions, rather than the billions of only twenty-eight days earlier.

The initial consensus indicated that North America was also in a state of complete turmoil. Both civil authority and the economy had totally collapsed. The Mayo Clinic in Scottsdale, Arizona sent in the most detailed report of what could be expected to be the norm across the nation.

The briefer, Dr. Tyler Deen said, via video feed from the CDC in Atlanta. "Mr. President, the Mayo Clinic in Scottsdale reports that the pandemic has killed 100% of patients over sixty years of age. They believe this will hold true across the U.S. The clinic also reported that anyone with pacemakers, and other specialty life-saving devices, also died. Perhaps, even more tragically, it appears that all children under the age of ten have also succumbed to the Mag-flu. Ultimately, sir, the death toll of hospitalized patients currently sits at around 95%."

Holcomb said, in an alarmed tone, "and they think this same situation will be countrywide?"

"Yes, sir," said Dr. Goldman, of the Scottsdale Mayo Campus. "The Clinic has also reported that those Staff Members under the age of sixty survived at a rate of roughly 25%, with half of those survivors becoming Mags.

"In third world countries, the death toll will be much higher than our own 75%. It seems likely that entire ethnic and cultural populations will simply disappear.

"Mr. President, the evidence coming in from our sister organizations around the world make it relatively clear that somewhere near seven-billion human beings lay dead, mostly in their beds. In just a few days the smell of decaying human flesh will become nearly unbearable.

"Soon, pets, rats, mice, well, anything that can feed off the dead will be doing so. With rats, first and foremost, the danger of disease will come into full bloom.

"Sir, I recommend that you remind, via whatever mass communications we have left, everyone to go to the city water box and turn off the water. Within a week that source will become mixed with sewage, and it will back up into any home with an open connection to city water. Considering the enormity of the death toll, this backup of sewage will create a horrendous opportunity for the rise of hygienic diseases. Mr. President, we must, therefore, make it clear to all survivors that they must take it upon themselves to move through their neighborhoods to shut off the water immediately.

"Survivors must also be warned about sanitation once the water is turned off. Waste must be buried well away from homes. Non-bottled water must be boiled for fifteen minutes before it will be safe to drink. Mr. President, these health concerns are the most pressing issues of our time, even more so than the Mag threat."

"Thank you, Dr. Deen, please see that your recommendations are forwarded to my Chief of Staff. We will at once place your directives on a repeating loop via Conelrad." said the President.

"Silas, let's hear your sad news." Mr. Silas Creed was the Vice President's Economic Advisor.

"Yes, sir, the economic portion of the briefing is simple and concise, there is no economy. Mr. President, the economy has completely crashed. Nothing, anywhere, is being transported, by any means. Starvation will soon begin to cause a second die-off beginning in the next few weeks, and there is nothing anyone can do to prevent it."

"But we have warehouses fully capable of feeding the surviving population for some time. Surely, we can feed our citizens until the farm produce comes to harvest. No, wait, sorry, that warehoused food may help local populations but if we can't transport it…"

"Yes, Mr. President, that is the situation in a nutshell. There are ample foodstuffs, but we have no means to transport them. Even if we had the trucks and drivers, they would be unable to refuel as the electric grid is now a cascading failure, with no coal or oil running the power plants."

President Holcomb asked if it was possible to restart the cold-fusion drives and restore power.

The COS, Simon Ward answered, "Sir, the technicians required to fire up the power plants are many, with highly specified training. We currently have no idea how many, if any, have survived. I'm sorry sir, but I don't believe that is possible at the present time. We will, of course, begin a search for these specialists, though, even if we are successful; it will still take months to even begin the process.

"The power grid is a fragile, complex assortment of many differing grid components that require men and computers to maintain the proper level of flow. Are there any linemen left? Where are they? Mr. President, bringing the grid back online may actually take years, even decades. Had we hardened and upgraded the grid over the last one-hundred and seventy-five years, well, maybe it would be a different story; we'll never know."

"Thank you, Silas," muttered a growingly despondent President.

The COS said, "Mr. President, with your approval, General Henry Morse will assume the role of Chairman of the Joint Chief's."

"Yes, of course," said President Vance Holcomb. Make it happen."

Then turning his gaze to General Morse, Holcomb said, "General, do we have any current status on surviving military forces?" asked President Holcomb.

"Sir," said General Morse, "so far our information is coming in slowly. I would have to say it is spotty at best. Those that have been able to make contact have outlined a very dark picture. The upper echelon of both the Officer and NCO ranks have been decimated. Of those officers in the Field and General Grades, which are from Major to General, it looks like the majority consists of Lieutenant Colonels. Currently, only a handful of Full Colonels and no General Officers have reported for duty.

"The NCO Corps has been hit even harder because the upper ranks tend to be older. I estimate the average enlisted survivor ranks to be the E-6 Staff Sergeants. I have ordered those surviving Officers and NCOs to begin establishing order and reorganization of a command structure.

"The reports that have come in indicate that the fighting has been savage. Initially, the Mags took a heavy toll, until our people were able to get weapons and sufficient ammunition. In those areas with a Conelrad connection, we believe may have fared somewhat better by listening to the emergency recording recommending they arm themselves before the Mags came out of hiding.

"Training Forts like Ft Benning apparently have the greatest number of survivors. I would guess that is due to the young men and women that were still in training. Those Forts and Bases also have the highest number of desertions, mostly from the Training Battalions. From the information gathered to date, the Mags tend to be very strong, very fast, and relentless in their attacks.

"Ultimately, Mr. President, we do not yet have sufficient data to even begin to make estimates of our military strength. I hope to have a clearer picture of our surviving assets within the next forty-eight hours.

"Additionally, Mr. President, once we have a better picture of our status, I would like to recommend that we reinforce Mount Weather and utilize it as an outpost for operations against the enemy. Should the appropriate resources be available, I would like to position a helicopter platoon to provide rapid deployment of forces from Fort Weather. The helos are already there, so personnel will be the deciding factor. Sir, that is all I have for now."

"Thank you, General," said the President, who placed his elbows on the table and began rubbing his temples in an attempt to stave off the migraine he felt coming on. After only a few seconds, Holcomb said to his COS, "Please draw up whatever paperwork is necessary to make Hank the Chairman of the Joint Chiefs. Then, please prepare a list of who is onsite with any qualification for the remaining necessary positions. Let's pare the government down a bit. Eliminate departments like HUD, Education, you know, right?"

"Of course, Mr. President," said the Chief of Staff. "That list is currently being fleshed out. I'll have it to you for your approval before tomorrow's morning brief.

"Good. Gentlemen, we have been handed a veritable double-decker garbage sandwich. Okay, now we must begin the long road back. Everyone will coordinate through the Chief of Staff.

"Hank, I want those projections of military strength, soonest. Once you have a picture of any given area, dispatch sufficient forces to find and secure storage warehouses, fuel storage farms, and water distribution sites. Establish a chit system for anyone living in the areas our forces have secured. Issue those chits to everyone in allotments to ensure food and transportation are covered. Make suggestions for other areas to protect and secure the populace. Reinstate local Police. Get the hospitals up and running.

"I know, Hank, I know, the list is unending, but I have one more job for you; seek out and destroy all Mags. No prisoners, either they die, or we die. You have one huge job, General, probably the most important one of all.

"Okay, electricity, gentlemen, I want every solar panel and residential wind turbine, not in private usage, in this country brought under our control, then begin installation first to the warehouses, then to government and military headquarters, and finally to the populace at large.

"General, I want it understood that any military member who tries to stake a claim to his own personal kingdom, is to be shot, following a five-minute Military Tribunal. The same goes for gangs, politicians, just bad guys in general.

"Simon; put this order in writing as a Presidential Order. We must cull those who are not in support of restoring order and improving the general welfare."

Looking around the table, the President asked, "Am I perfectly clear, here? No exceptions. All prisons are to be put on lockdown. No prisoners will be released into the general population. Any remaining staff will be federalized and utilized to support the local police."

"Sir," interrupted the COS, "I want it perfectly understood that it is your intention to close all prisons and abandon them, with inmates locked down. Is this correct?"

"Yes, Simon, that is correct. I will not authorize the release of any criminal element into the public domain who, even potentially, might prey upon law-abiding citizens. Most are already dead, and the rest will join the deceased in another three or four days. There will be no pardon for anyone currently confined to Federal, State, County, or City jail."

"Thank you, Mr. President, I apologize for my interruption, but I wanted it made clear that you, no, make that we, will not further endanger the good people that are now so desperately trying to deal with the current struggle just to survive."

Norman Freeman, the FEMA Director interrupted, saying, "What? Sir, you can't do that, why it's tantamount to murder. If we can't take care of them, then we must set them free. It's just not right to let them die, like, like rats."

"Norman," said an irritated President, "my order stands. No prisoners will be turned out to prey on others."

President Holcomb then asked Admiral Harley Huxley to report on the status of both the Ocean Going and the Space Defense Force.

"Yes, sir. Mr. President, the sea-going fleets are all running on skeleton crews. Arming the sailors was the difference between having floating hulks full of death, and, at least, minimal crews. Our Carriers are having the most difficulty as the force needed to operate them is significant. Those that were unable to make U.S. ports prior to Holly Thorne's arrival are limping in. The question is, do we have sufficient personnel to operate even a modicum of a functioning Naval Surface Force? Honestly, sir, I just don't know.

"Our Submarines were all able to submerge before Holly Thorne's arrival. We have received replies from each, and they report no infections. I have ordered them to remain submerged until we know that the pandemic has passed, and the air is clear.

"The Space Defense Force, which departed several weeks ago, have met up with Admiral Scott King's fleet and are still *en route* to the Mars Colony at Red Sands. They report no infections and anticipate joining the Mars Colony in six days, on 9 April."

"Thank you, Admiral, it's good to know we still have our subs. I suspicion our surface fleet is scragged, without sufficiently trained personnel to even perform scheduled maintenance. Admiral Huxley, once you have a hard count of personnel and their respective technical skills, please try to reopen the necessary training facilities."

"Yes, sir, of course," said a despondent Admiral Huxley. "Sir, reopening the necessary schools may prove inconsequential as replacement parts, and food stores will run out with little chance of replacement."

"I know, Admiral, I know, but we must start somewhere, and this seems to me like square one. Getting spare parts may never come back online, but we have to try.

"Our population may now only sport a few tens of millions, but many will migrate to the previous centers of production and our ports. They will need jobs, and we can help there.

"I am extremely concerned about the surviving farming communities. They must be helped and supported in any way possible. We must encourage survivors to take up farming. Ultimately, only those who farm can save the nation."

Vance Holcomb then looked directly at Silas Creed, the Economic Advisor. He said, "Silas, I hope you just made some notes. You have made it quite clear that we have no economy, all right, then let's get off our dead asses and get to work on a new one."

"FEMA," said Vance in a rising voice, "Mr. Freeman, we need to know how many Americans have survived and what their job skills are. Let's discover a way to answer those questions, then begin contracted relocations. I hope you caught the term contracted relocations. Norman, there will be no FEMA Camps that utilize forced labor. Anyone choosing to leave the safety of the camps will be free to do so. If I ever discover that any of your people have mistreated any American, I will have them shot, and you will be dropped off at the nearest Mag nest. Am I clear?"

"Of course, Mr. President, but you certainly did not need to make such threats."

"Mr. Freeman, nothing I just said to you were threats. They were promises. Promises that I intend to keep. Simon, belay that order to ditch the Education position. I want a nominee who will get going on the three Rs, with emphasis on Trade Schools. We don't need philosophers right now. We need workers who can produce tangible, needed products. I will not abide slave labor. If someone does not want to work, they will receive no support from us, and they will be escorted to the gate. Those who wish to rebuild their lives will have the opportunity to do so."

President Holcomb added, "Well, there it is. All right, I could go on for a seeming eternity, but this will do for today. I want a viable plan of action from each of you in five days, ready for you to brief at the 0900 meet-up. You all have your assignments, now let's get to them. Simon, you and Hank remain after the meeting."

Once the room had been cleared, President Holcomb said, "General, I truly hope you have someone to take on the job of Anti-Mag Field Operations."

"Yes, sir, I do, Colonel Tom Merritt, Commanding the 175th Ranger Regiment. General Howard informed me that he is currently a survivor at Fort Benning. He is the man for the job and is on the General Officer's promotion list. With your permission, sir, I would like to see him promoted immediately to the rank of Major General. Two stars will, most likely, make him the senior Military Officer on the surface."

"Good plan, I approve. Simon, make it legal for posterity. Hank, we need to get a command structure to the Mount Weather folks. There are too many Rangers twiddling their thumbs waiting for leadership. I know there are Marines closer, but I'd rather have Rangers commanding Rangers. Let's get them into the fight."

"Yes, sir, I'll get with General Merritt soonest."

"Hank, I also promote you to General of the Army, via Presidential Order, and effective at once. I'll bet we have some machinists who could whip up some five-star collar pins.

"Now, General, and you too Simon, I want to drive this home to you and to everyone else; there is to be no quarter in the Mag War. Require General Merritt to hunt these Mag creatures down, hunt them down and kill them, kill them all."

General Henry H. Morse thanked the President and realizing he had been excused, saluted his Commander-In-Chief before departing.

"Simon, create a force designed to find and secure all gold that is not held privately. Can you do this?"

"Yes, Vance, but even though I don't know exactly how we'll go about it, I will learn and make it happen."

"I have no doubt about it," said Holcomb. "I also want to quickly discuss with you that I want you to become my Vice, but right now, I need a Chief of Staff more than a VPOTUS. However, I'm sure that once things get rolling, that need will change. You okay with that?"

"Sir, you know I have no aspirations for any job more than I have right now, but having said that, I know you are correct about the needs of reconstruction. So, yes, Mr. President, I will accept when the time is right."

Holcomb looked relieved as he said, "Thank you, Simon, I'm glad you understand, and that you will accept. Now, it's time to shake a leg, come on, let's get at it."

Simon smiled at his friend of fifty years before saying, "Vance, you have laid out an epic undertaking, but epic or not, it just has to happen."

"I know, Simon, but this is a pickle, a real sour pickle. I doubt if we'll be back to a fully functioning government in our lifetime, but since the buck stops here, here is where we'll start. Any questions?"

"Yes, sir," said Simon, "a couple of million, but I'll need to sort them out before I hit you with them. You did well, Vance. I am proud of the way you have taken the proverbial bull by the horns, and of the course of actions to set recovery in motion, yes, sir, very proud.

"Oh, one more thing. I intend to keep an eye on that rat bastard Freeman. He was really pissed when he left, and I have to tell you, Vance, I don't trust him, never have. He may need replacing."

The President looked at his friend and said, "If he doesn't shape up, then ship him out and sooner rather than later. He might make a good example for everyone else."

"Vance," said the COS in a comforting voice, "we might fail, but we can't quit, we won't quit, or we'll die first. Once the plans are in from the department heads, and the updates on our military, you and I should sit down and look at this conundrum from a micro-view."

"Good idea, go ahead and put it on the calendar."

4 APRIL 2118,
BIOMEYER HEALTH FITNESS CENTER
1525 CLIFTON RD NE FL 5, ATLANTA, GA 30322

Physical Therapist Warren and his brother Clansman, Kim, continued moving in an easterly direction, directly on a course to the Main Entrance to the new CDC, Level 5 Complex.

CHAPTER FIVE

THE GENETIC MARKER

5 APRIL 2118
NATIONAL GUARD ARMORY
MOUNDSVILLE, WV

Jake and his team took turns looking at the ten, or so, Monsters wandering the street in front of the National Guard Armory. These creatures walked upright, with no knuckle-dragging that they could see.

Jake recorded the Mag activity, both by video and recorded notes. He thought that one of the most interesting rituals of Mag meeting Mag was the sniffing of each other's head and neck. At times they would form packs, while other times they would simply continue their search for a closer relationship. Jake surmised that the clothing worn by the Mags might be a clue to the clan encounter and formation. He made note that on two occasions, he saw former Police Officers joining forces.

Jake also noted that the Mags had been killing rabbits, dogs, cats, and whatever else came across their path. They were also apparently excellent hunters, though this confused Jake as to how they would so instinctively be so successful at garnering food.

"Gale, there has to be some genetic marker or ancestral memory that allows them to be so successful in the hunt."

"Yes, what else could it possibly be. Mags certainly don't have available parents to teach them such an important skill. You know, I wonder if they are developing a hunter class derived from those Mags that were hunters when they were human."

"Now, that's an interesting idea. I'll add that thought to the notes for the CDC. And speaking of the CDC, we need to contact them before the power goes completely out. I think I'll try the telephone in the Orderly Room. Who knows, it might still work. Maybe we'll get some help in getting out of here," said Jake.

The team was gathered, and all went to the Orderly Room. Jake picked up a landline phone and was greatly pleased to hear a dial-tone. He hung the phone back up and began searching for a telephone alert tree in an attempt to contact someone from the Armory.

"Here it is," said an excited Ibrahim Shah, "it was under the Company Clerk's Ink Blotter."

"Good job, Ham. Okay, let's start at the top, with the Commanding Officer (CO)." Jake dialed the number for the CO and got no answer. He then went through the list of Officers but came up empty with each.

Next came the First Sergeant who answered the phone after only one ring. "First Sergeant Israel Sanders, who is calling?"

The Dig Team began jumping up and down in joy at the realization that contact was made with the NCO that really ran the company.

"First Sergeant Sanders, my name is Professor Jacob Abraham. My Dig Team and I, what's left of it, are still at the Armory. I have some information that I believe may be important to the CDC, but with no information service working, I have no idea how to get their number. Can you help?"

"All right, the government phone book is located in the top filing cabinet drawer. It's the one with four drawers. Do you see it?" asked the First Sergeant.

"Yes, hold on, please. Frank, check it out."

Frank Lusk, Donna's arch enemy tried to open the drawer but found the cabinet had a long metal rod reaching from a loop with a padlock attached. The rod passed through each drawer handle and ended with another loop and hook that attached it to the floor.

"Sorry, Doc, but the cabinet is locked up tight as a drum."

The First Sergeant overheard the conversation between Jake and Frank. When Jake came back online, he heard the Top Sergeant say, "Sir, a spare key is located in the top, middle drawer of my desk. It is also locked, but you should have no real problem in prying it open. It's okay, do it now."

Dave sat before the Top's desk and taking his Bowie Knife quickly pried the drawer open. He quickly found a set of keys and offered them to Jake, who signaled Frank to hold on to them.

"All right, Top, we have your key set. There must be twenty keys on this ring. Do we have to try them all?"

"No, look on the top, right side of the cabinet, and you will see a number. The cabinet keys have a number on them. Match the numbers, and you're in."

"Are you Prior Service, Doc?" asked the First Sergeant.

"Yes, a long time ago. How did you know?"

"You called me Top, I wouldn't expect a civilian to know about that moniker."

"Oh, yeah, I guess that would be a dead give-a-way. Top, is there a way for us to get a couple of vehicles running? We have a van, but I would be much more comfortable with a lightly armored scout vehicle with a Squad Machine Gun mounted on top."

"I really think the info I have will be important to the CDC," said Jake.

"Yes, but I will have to meet you at the Armory. The keys to the Motor Park and Vehicles are locked in the Company safe. I can get us in a couple of vehicles, but the MGs will have no ammo. We weren't scheduled to go to Summer Training until Mid-June, so the small-arms ammo hasn't yet been delivered. Unfortunately, we aren't an ammunition storage facility. We have the weapons, just no ammo."

"Look, give me an hour. I'm pretty sure that I can get to you, but, please, keep an eye out for my arrival. I may need to be let in quickly. I'll put on a uniform and be right there. Professor are you safe? Do you have any weapons?" asked the First Sergeant.

"Yes, on both counts. Be aware that several Mags are wandering around. I think they are in the process of creating clans, so, please be careful."

"Roger that, I'll get there as quickly as I can," said First Sergeant Izzy Sanders.

"Roger, Top," said Jake, "we've got no other place to go until you get here."

Once the connection was broken, Jake briefed his team on the conversation. Jake began looking at the Military phone book. He quickly realized that the instructions were so alien to civilian auto-connect assist modes that he quickly gave up and decided to wait for Sanders to arrive. In the meantime, three team members began packing up the gear. The remaining three were put on guard duty; one at each entrance and one going from room to room checking to make sure that no windows were broken.

4 APRIL 2118
HOTEL ST. MICHAEL
GURLEY ST,
PRESCOTT, ARIZONA

Cindy Sharp became aware of crashing sounds of destruction coupled with the howls of still more monsters. She was three steps from the stairwell when the door of Room 300 burst open as the Mag threw his body crashing against a door that could have been opened by the simple downward motion of the door's handle.

The Mag fell to the floor on top of the door which had come completely off its hinges. He quickly looked around and roared a challenge to Cindy as he lept to his feet with amazing speed. With equal speed she raised her pistol and fired two times, striking the Mag in the chest.

Cindy had noticed three things about this monstrosity, he was very strong, very fast, and his eye orbitals were rectangular rather than oval.

As an afterthought, she also noticed that this thing was wearing only boxer underwear and a Tee-shirt.

A stray thought crossed her mind; Zombies? No, these things are far more dangerous.

Cindy carefully made her way down the five flights of stairs. She utilized her training in clearing a building, weapon held straight out and advancing in a crouch. There were no further encounters until she reached the lobby and found three human bodies. The initial evidence indicated that each had been killed by a blunt force trauma to the head.

The bodies of what appeared to have been a family, fortunate enough to survive the pandemic intact, found death at the hands of raging monsters. Their bodies lay in a tragic heap, the result of a sudden and terrifying attack.

Cindy was a warrior, and this senseless murder scene did not cause her to fear. No, it angered her down to the marrow of her bones. At that exact moment, Cindy knew she would dedicate her life to the eradication of these monsters, no matter how long it took.

Upon opening the front entrance of the St. Michael Hotel, Cindy began hearing screams and sporadic gunfire. Good, she thought, others are beginning to fight back.

The gunfire which roared and expelled sudden death was somewhat short-lived in this, the first day of the Mag Invasion. In the first hours, armed Arizonans took a heavy toll of the invading horde. Soon, however, the tide began to turn as the humans began to run out of ammunition. Many began making their way to gun stores, but the ones to survive long enough to get more ammunition were mostly prior military.

Cindy replaced the magazine in her pistol, not because it was empty, but because she wanted to meet any threat with a full magazine. She took stock of her ammunition reserves as she made her way to her car.

As she opened the car's trunk to retrieve her reserve ammo, a shout of rage screamed out a challenge. Cindy turned quickly to see two Mags running toward her with raised clubs in their hands. Quickly she fired four shots into the chests of the attackers which dropped them in their tracks. From their clothing, they had both been policemen.

Before getting into her car, Cindy retrieved the weapons, ammunition, and radios from the dead. It struck her as oddly funny that these two had once been men whose job was to protect and serve.

Retreating to the minimal safety of her car, Cindy spoke to her Garmin GPS to get directions to the nearest police station. She then checked the radios taken from her assailants and discovered that the batteries of both were depleted.

As she arrived at the nearest police station, Cindy carefully exited her car, then locked the doors. She made her way into the station, and upon finding it deserted, she searched, and found, the weapons locker, which, to her surprise, was standing open. Once inside Cindy began stacking weapons and ammunition near the outer door. Her plan was to take them to her car and then begin to make her War Plan.

Cindy had four fully-auto ARs in her arms as she made her way back to the entrance. Upon entering the main lobby, she found herself facing someone standing in the doorway. Coming from the darkened back rooms, she was unable to see anything but a black silhouette fronting the sunlight streaming in through the door.

Cindy threw the weapons at the figure and reached for her own weapon, when she heard, "Wait, don't shoot. I'm not one of them."

Now aiming her pistol at the center of the intruder's chest she said, "Raise your hands high, then step into the room, and away from the door, so I can get a clear visual on you."

"Yes, ma'am," said the stranger who raised his hands and stepped away from the sunlit doorway. "Can I lower my hands now?"

"No," said Cindy, "keep them high until my eyes can clearly see you. She next said, "All right, lower your hands and empty your pockets. Do you have any weapons on you?"

The young man, in his mid-twenties, asked no questions as he emptied his pockets. He said, "No ma'am, no weapons. That's why I came here. My Platoon Sergeant always said that in an emergency I should check out the local police station for weapons."

"Platoon Sergeant? Are you military?"

"No, ma'am, not anymore, I did a three-year enlistment as a Mortar-man," said the man. "You seem to know what you are about. Were you military?"

Before answering any questions, Cindy directed him to back up while she went through his pocket items. She saw nothing threatening so she said, "All right, lower your hands. Yes, I am retired Army, twenty-five years. I don't think we'll find any mortars here, though."

"No, ma'am, but every soldier is a basic infantryman, so, I came here to get weapons to take on that role. Oh, my name is James, well, Jim, Jim Mason."

At just that instant two Mags burst through the door and before their eyes could adjust, Cindy dropped them to the ground, dead. She then turned back to Jim and said in a voice that belied the fact that she had just killed two Mags, said, "Nice to meet you, Jim, I'm Cindy Sharpe. Do you have family, here, Jim?"

"Holy crap," Jim Mason nearly shouted, "you just killed them and continued the introductions like nothing happened. What are you, some kinda Delta Force, or something?"

"Nope, I flew Gunships," said Cindy, "These things are just like Black-Widow Spiders, you see one, you squish it and move on. Now, about family?"

"Oh, not anymore. The flu took my folks and girlfriend. I wish I had time to mourn them, but right now, staying alive takes precedence. I'll mourn later."

Cindy did not fail to notice that despite Jim's bravado, there was much hurt in his eyes.

Cindy said, "Go ahead and find your choice for weapons. Then we'll load them up, say, what are you driving?"

"Yes, ma'am, I was raised on a small horse ranch over in Skull Valley, so, of course, I got me a 4X4 Dodge Ram 1500, why?"

"Why? Well, because I'm driving a Toyota Camry, so we'll take yours," said Cindy, "and damn it, stop calling me ma'am."

"Yes, ma'am, er, I mean, Cindy. Okay, yeah, we should take mine. Dang it, Cindy, I was raised on sir and ma'am. So, you'll just have ta' bear with me on that, okay?"

Cindy liked this kid and said, "Yeah, sure, but don't run it in the ground, huh?"

Jimmy smiled back at Cindy, saying, "Yes'm, do you have a plan?"

"Yes, I surely do. The first thing is to go to that radio station, KFNA. Do you know where it is?"

"Oh, sure," said Jim, "It's right next to Costco. I shop there a lot, and that's also where I get my diesel."

"Well, hot diggity, let's roll before we get interrupted again."

"Sure, but why the radio station?" asked Jim.

"Just hang on, Jim, stick with me, and you might learn some things."

"Yes'm."

Cindy felt bad about stomping on Jim's question, so she said, "Okay, phase one is to contact the DJ and get him to make the announcement that we have taken the Walmart, the one just past Lowe's. We put out the word that we are looking for volunteers to join a small Militia Group."

Jim interrupted saying, "Militia Group, what Militia Group?"

"You and me, come on Jim, stay with me now, remember I did say a small group. Oh, yeah, and stop interrupting."

"Yes ma'am, I like it. Sorry to interrupt, please go on."

Cindy groaned a deep sigh at the ma'am thing but decided to just give up on it. She said, "Thank you, now, as I was saying before being so rudely interrupted. After we get the word out, we ask if the DJ has access to a remote setup. If he does, we convince him to join up. Since there are two of them at the station, we will have doubled the size of the Prescott Militia.

"While this DJ Foote gets his gear ready, you and I will head to the Walmart, clear it, then set up shop. Phase two is enlisting others to join us. So, we had better hope that there are folks out there who are listening to the radio, and the quicker, the better. Even if the radio thing doesn't pan out the Walmart store will act as a natural magnet for both survivors and Mags. Of course, if we don't find some help, and soon, we are going to get very, very tired."

It took about forty minutes to clean out the police station of weapons, ammunition, mace, body armor, helmets face guards, and shields. As the last of the equipment was loaded onto Jim's pickup, Cindy said, "You ready to saddle up, soldier?"

"Yes, ma'am, uh, Cindy, I'm ready. Let's go and kick some Mag ass."

"Well, all right," smiled Cindy, "good plan. You know, Jim, I think you'll do."

5 APRIL 2118
ARMORY PARKING LOT
MOUNDSVILLE, WV

Sanders drove into the Armory parking lot forty minutes after speaking with Jake. The sound of his truck's engine caught the attention of two Mags who were father and son. They, at once, began advancing toward this beast. By the time the pick-up engine was shut down, two Mags with clubs were seen watching the truck. It quickly became clear that the Mags were in awe of this monster that spit out another creature, that in some strange way resembled themselves.

The two Mags were so frightened of this monster, they decided not to attack such a huge beast. Having seen many others of these sleeping beasts, they decided to quietly make their way home to communicate with the other members of their new clan.

As they made their retreat, both Mags made their best efforts to give these huge beasts as wide a berth as possible, however, near the edge of the lot the trailing Mag passed a small Volkswagen Beetle. With safety, only steps away, he struck the headlight with an aluminum baseball bat. The blow shattered the light, and the young Mag ran for cover.

Once they were safely hidden, the older Mag struck his son in the chest with his fist as a warning not to awaken sleeping monsters. As they peered back at the VW, both were surprised to see that the blow had blinded what they perceived as a child of the pick-up trucks just before and behind the VW.

They were surprised to discover that the monster clan had not awakened. Surely, thought the elder, the young one must have been killed by the blow to its eye.

This single action was the beginning of Mag theory that a blow to the eye of the beast would kill it. That evening, over the cooking fire, the males of the clan discussed, through grunts and pantomime, the bravery of the young Mag that killed a monster.

During this discussion, one sound was used many times. Soon the guttural utterance of *Lha* would become a word meaning no. The learning curve of these reincarnated Mags was impressive.

5 APRIL 2118
RADIO STATION KFNA, 99.9 FM
PRESCOTT, AZ

The drive to the radio station took only seven or eight minutes to reach KFNA. Jim parked the truck directly in front of the station. Both Cindy and Jim cautiously exited the pickup, locked the doors, then began searching the perimeter. The area proved to be clear of Mags, and upon going to the main entrance, they found the door locked and barricaded.

"Well, crap," said Cindy, "there's no way they'll be able to hear us, and yelling may well draw the attention of unwanted critters. You got any ideas, Jim?"

Jim's face brightened and suggested that they use Cindy's portable radio and listen to hear if the DJ offers a telephone number. Cindy patted him on the shoulder and said, "Smarter than the average bear, Jimmy, yep, smarter than the average bear."

She took the radio from her backpack and turned it on. The time was just after the top of the hour, and both listened for a phone number. The DJ finished his news roundup, then said, "If anyone out there hears me, please call 928-315-1589."

Jim wrote down the number and using his phone called the station. When the DJ answered, Cindy took the phone and explained that she and Jim were at the front door. The Sound Engineer quickly ran to the door and saw Cindy and Jim. He quickly moved the barricade and opened the door. The DJ came around the corner and introduced himself and his Engineer.

Cindy explained the plan to take the Walmart and for Mr. DJ Foote to put out the word about the Militia's takeover of Walmart. DJ and the Engineer, David Painter, reported that the station did have a remote unit and would be most pleased to join an active Militia. The Walmart would provide pretty much everything they would need to survive for some time. It was agreed that DJ and Dave would fire up the remote and meet them at the Walmart in about an hour. He also said that he would make the first announcement of the Prescott Militia's new quarters.

On the way to Walmart, Jim asked Cindy if she thought that DJ realized that the Prescott Militia only had two members. Cindy turned to Jim with a smile and said, "Not a chance. I figured that was an unimportant detail, and he'll find out soon enough." This caused them both to laugh loud and hard, something they had not done since the comet's light show.

5 APRIL 2118
ARMORY MAIN ENTRANCE
MOUNDSVILLE, WV

First Sergeant Sanders was hurriedly brought inside the building, but before proper introductions could be made, Jake directed Sanders to the two Mags that were watching Sanders' truck. They continued to watch and witnessed the younger Mag smash the headlight of a VW Beetle, then run for his life.

"Holy crap," said Gale, "did you see that?"

Jake didn't respond, as he was busy recording both audio and video of the incident. After the Mag duo departed the area, introductions were made all around.

Sanders asked Jake if he lost any team members, family, or friends.

"Yes," said Jake, "we began our archaeology dig with a compliment of twenty-two. Of those team members still with us, none have been able to contact any family. Now, we are seven. I'm not sure about family and probably will never know. Most are gone, except for and Aunt Bernice and a few cousins. How about yourself?"

Sanders looked down at the floor. It was obvious that he was shaken by the question.

"First Sergeant, I'm sorry, perhaps we should change the subject, at least for now."

"Yes," said Sanders, "It's still too fresh. We were all together when the illness struck. Yes, later, thanks." He perked up somewhat, as though he had shut a file drawer of memories. First Sergeant Izzy Sanders was a soldier who had seen several deployments to Berzerkistan. His training and life as a warrior had allowed him to compartmentalize the hurt which tore at his soul, but his eyes had lost their shine.

"Well, First Sergeant…"

"Please, Professor," said Sanders, "call me Izzy, or Israel, I'm happy with either one."

Jake smiled at his new friend and said, "Thank you, Izzy, and please call me Jake. Have you been able to make contact with any members of your unit?"

"Yes, a few, but they all live more than fifty miles away. Of those few, only ten were willing and able to report for duty. I told them to stay with family for now and to offer their services to any local government departments that might still be functioning. Did you have any luck with the CDC?"

"Top, I hate to admit it, but the phone network was just too complicated for me. I decided to wait for you and allow my team to try to reach family. This team of mine may be young in age, but they are all West Virginians and are coping well. Two of us are Army Veteran's; myself and Frank Lusk. We both had one deployment to the Sandbox. We got out as E-5s."

"Good, good, do you have any long guns?"

"No, all of our weapons are sidearms, but we do have quite a bit of ammo," said Jake."

"Good report, now, shall we get your call to the CDC?"

Three minutes later the CDC Operator answered the call. "CDC, please state the nature of your call," came a curt sounding Operator.

"Hello," said Jake, "my name is Professor Jacob Abraham. I Chair the Archaeology and Paleontology Department at West Virginia University. I have information concerning the physical transition from Human to Mag. Put me through to your Director," said an equally curt Jacob.

"Hold one, please," said the Operator in a much more conciliatory tone.

"Hello, this is Doctor Tyler Deen. I understand you have some information concerning the transition period of the Mags. Where are you currently located, Professor Abrams?"

"Sir, I am in Moundsville, West Virginia, and my name is Abraham."

Deen said, "My apologies, Professor Abraham, I'll just change that in my notes, here. All right, now, please tell me about your information."

"My Dig Team and I have observed the turn of one male and one female from Human to Mag. We made regular notes, written, recorded, and videoed. Would you like to have them?"

Deen now seemed excited at the possibility of obtaining this information, especially the video portion. "Yes, of course, absolutely, oh, my, yes. How do you propose to get them to us? We can arrange pickup if you are unable to come here."

"Doctor, do you have a secure way to receive this information?"

"Yes, absolutely," said Deen, "but if you come in to our facility, we can give you a physical exam and provide safety."

Jake wanted no part of becoming a test subject for CDC Researchers. He said, "No, Doc, that doesn't work for me, but I will ask the survivors of my team to see if they are interested. Here is my proposal; I will place all of our data into your secure drop-box and depart."

"I see," replied Deen, "all right, I agree to your terms. How may I contact you?"

Jake told him that for the next four hours he could be reached at the Armory phone. After that, his group would be out of pocket until they arrived at the CDC facility. Since the roads were almost totally free of vehicles, Jake believed the trip of 650 miles should take no more than ten or eleven hours by driving straight through and cycling drivers. Deen suggested that the CDC could send an airplane to pick the team up and fly them down to Atlanta. Again, this was not an idea, or trap, that Jake was willing to accept.

"No," said Jake, "there are Mags everywhere, and I do not intend for us to be trapped in an unsecured airport."

"Doctor Deen, you will have the data at some point in the next twenty-four hours. Goodbye, sir," said Jake as he broke the connection.

Jake then turned to his team and said, "Well, there you have it. They want the data, and I have a suspicion they want us for research. So, here's your chance for safety. If you would like to join the CDC folks, let me know by the time we get to Atlanta."

The First Sergeant then said, "We have vehicles and fuel. I suggest we mount machine guns on each vehicle, even though they will be just for show since we have no ammunition. Showing them might keep any bad guys out there from trying to take the vehicles away from us.

"I also think it would be a good idea to pull out right after dark. Mags have to sleep, too, and eight or nine hours of travel will put us near Atlanta by sun up."

5 APRIL 2118, 1800
CDC
SECURE LEVEL 5 LABS BUILDING
1600 CLIFTON RD NE, ATLANTA, GA 30329

Dr. Deen was both excited and frustrated at the conditions set forth by this Professor Abraham. He decided that he must quickly inform the

President's Chief of Staff. Deen dialed the personal cellphone of the COS.

Seeing that the incoming call was from the CDC, Simon Ward quickly answered, "Ward here. Tyler, I hope you are calling to tell me that you've made a breakthrough," said an anxious COS.

"Hello, Simon," said Deen, "unfortunately we do not have a breakthrough, but we did get a huge break that may well lead to one. I was just contacted by a Professor Jacob Abraham, the Chair of the Archaeology Department at West Virginia University. He reports that he is currently in Moundsville, West Virginia and has data and video on the transition from Human to Mags on both a male and female.

"Simon, we need that data, now. Abraham was unwilling to be picked up at the Moundsville Airport. He said that he and his team would be departing in the next few hours from their current undisclosed location. They plan to drive through the night and deliver the data in the next twenty-four hours.

"Simon, we need, not only the data, but I would like to take possession of these seven people for physical exams and further study. Can you make this happen?"

The President's Chief of Staff's voice became both sharp and commanding. He said, "Doctor Deen, did the President not make it clear to you that no one would be held against their will? Is there some way I can be assured that you understand his directive?"

Deen quickly changed his demeanor and replied, "No, sir, I absolutely understand. I will, of course, adhere to the President's directive, please accept my apologies, I guess I did get carried away."

"Yes, Doctor, you most certainly did. I also assure you that this call is being recorded and I will make certain that it is kept in safe keeping. I will not make your request known to the President unless, or until, you decide to disregard President Holcomb's directive. Understood, Doctor?"

"Yes, sir, completely understood. I assure you that there will be no violation of President Holcomb's guidance," said a contrite Deen.

Now, the COS sounded angry as he said, "Damn it, Deen, the President did not give guidance on this issue. He gave a directive. Damn, what the hell is the matter with you?"

Deen was now concerned that he might lose his job and be tossed out into the open pandemic filled air.

"No, no, please, I didn't mean that to sound like I did not understand his meaning. It was simply a poor choice of semantics. It will not happen again."

"All right, Tyler," said a mollified Simon Ward, "your apology is understood and accepted. Shall we get back to a more congenial discussion?"

"Yes, Simon, I would like that. I hope you know that I am on-board with the President's path moving forward."

"Thank you, Tyler, I'll get back to you soon. Please be sure to keep me informed of any new developments. Goodbye."

Before Deen could say his own goodbyes, the line went dead. Deen made an obscene gesture toward the phone and said, in a low voice, "What an asshole."

CHAPTER SIX

GUNFIRE

5 APRIL 2118

WALMART

PRESCOTT, AZ

Cindy was thrilled to find the parking lot empty, and even more pleased to find four semi-trucks backed up to the loading docks. The huge steel doors were down and locked, another piece of luck. She directed Jim to park right in front of the right side Main Entrance.

"Well, there's another break, the doors are still intact. It also looks like we are just a bit ahead of the power curve. Everyone else must be busy either fighting or dying. All right Jimmy, look sharp Soldier, I just found you, and I'd rather not have anyone other than me kill you, okay?"

"Yes, ma'am, but why would you kill me?"

Cindy smiled and said, "Most likely for calling me, ma'am."

Jim smiled but did not respond. Cindy believed in being prepared for any old apocalypse and pulled a set of lock picks from her seemingly bottomless pack.

Jim was surprised at the picks, and he asked, "Cindy, do you know how to use those picks?"

"Son, let me ask you something; why would I have a set of lock picks if I didn't pay a locksmith to teach me how to use 'em? Fortunately, the power is off so no alarm. We'll rip that out after we're all settled in."

"Why bother?" asked Jim, if the power is off. Oh, wait, yeah, generators. Damn, Cindy, you are one smart cookie."

"Thanks, Jim, now let's go on in and clear the building. We don't want to walk up to a Mag that had been a Manager with a set of keys, who was here when he turned, now would we?"

"No, ma'…um, Cindy, good thinking."

She swung the door open, and both stepped through in combat mode.

"Well, damn," whispered Cindy, "I didn't really expect it to be this dark. She reached into her pack and pulled out a night vision monocle."

"Dang, Cindy, is there anything you don't have in that pack?"

"Yes, foolishly, I didn't plan on finding a partner who didn't have a pack just like mine. Now, shut up and stay behind me. We'll go to sporting goods first. Walmart does sell night vision monoculars, you know."

"Well, hot dog, I did not know that."

Upon reaching the sporting goods department, Cindy quickly found a monocular that would strap onto Jim's helmet.

"Cindy, I don't have a helmet. Say, would a football helmet work?"

"Yep," said Cindy, "right this way," and with helmet, monocular, and batteries in hand, Cindy led them back out of the store and into the sunlight. In only a few minutes, Jim was hooked up and ready to return to the darkened store.

With both of them utilizing the night vision monoculars it took about an hour to clear the store. They had just exited when DJ and Dave rolled up in a nearly new remote broadcast vehicle.

DJ got out of the van and said, "Is it clear?"

"It sure is. Say, Dave, do you think you can get the generator cranked up, so we can get some light inside?"

"Sure thing, can you spare some of your troops to provide security while I get it up and running?"

"Can do, Jim, help the man out."

"Really, just one man. How about getting a couple more out here to help him?"

Cindy looked straight-faced at Dave and said, "Others, what others?"

DJ and Dave both took on a look of near panic when DJ asked, "Cindy, just how many men do you have in this militia of yours?"

"Oh, that," smiled Cindy, "that would be four, for right now, but your broadcasts will bring in many others."

"WHAT?" snapped DJ, "only four? I think we'd better meet them before we go any further."

"Oh, sure," said Cindy, "Dave, my name is Cindy Sharpe, my friend here is Jim Mason, and this is DJ Foote. Okay, introductions are over, let's get to work."

"What? No, wait! Do you mean that your militia is just you and Mason?"

Cindy smiled and said, "Of course not, there's the two of you. Okay, DJ, seriously now, consider this, are you better off here, or stuck back in your studio with little food or water?"

DJ thought for a second, while his surprise and horror began to subside and reality set in. "Yeah, well, here, I suppose, but how can we hold this huge store with just us?"

"My friend," said Cindy, "it will be difficult to impossible for us to survive unless you get off your ass and get that radio up and running. Right now, there are many Arizonans willing to fight. They only need to know that we are here and that we intend to fight back. So, the sooner you get to work, the sooner we'll grow this force and take our town back."

DJ thought for another second and said, "Dave, get that genny up and running, now. We've got a show to get out."

5 APRIL 2118, DAWN
CLIFTON RD NE FL 5, ATLANTA, GA 30322

The two Mags from the Biomeyer Rehab Center took shelter the previous night in one of the nearby buildings. They had hoped to spend the night in relative safety. Both Mags lamented that they had none of the essentials to build a fire. There was simply no way for either of them to understand how to use the cigarette lighter that lay on the counter just inches away from their chosen spot to rest.

Some form of ancestral memory caused the Mags to awaken at dawn, on 5 April. Both were ravenous and needed food.

They left the security of their previous night and began hunting for something edible. Both Mags carried a fist-sized rock in the hope that they might be able to kill some small animal with a fastball.

The sun was just peeking over the horizon when Warren spotted a rabbit just twenty feet ahead. The silly rabbit sat frozen in the hope that these new animals would not notice him.

Warren and Kim both froze in place before taking aim and throwing their stones. They were close, but the rabbit was spooked by the sudden arm movements of his assailants.

The Mags began grunting and complaining about their missed chance at something to eat. Once their hissy fit was finished, they continued to the east. In only a few minutes the two Mags came across another rabbit. Kim cocked his head and for several seconds looked at what would hopefully become his breakfast.

He motioned for Warren to remain where he stood. Kim then slowly backed up a few steps before easing around to the rabbit's left flank. The rabbit remained perfectly still but kept his main attention on Warren. This time only Kim threw his rock while Warren looked on. The stone hit the rabbit in the neck, breaking it. Both Mags then charged up to their kill and enjoyed a bloody breakfast.

Mags could become tacticians on some level.

The two Mags were still far from sated but were pleased to have something in their stomachs. They continued their easterly movement but saw nothing edible. Nothing, until they came upon a cave with a large opening. Both Mags sniffed the air and discovered the scent of a dead wild hog. Following their noses, they soon saw the carcass that was just inside the opening.

They immediately went into stealth mode to make sure that this kill had not been made by a Cave Bear or Sabre Tooth. Smelling the air only produced two scents; the hog, and the same strange scent they experienced yesterday morning in that first cave.

Slowly the two Mags approached the hog. The movement of a remote camera went unnoticed by them. Finally, both Mags slipped into the cave's opening, which slammed shut behind them, and a blue gas filled the cave which put them to sleep.

The Mags had no memory of the five-story drop of the elevator to the secured Level 5 chamber. The CDC had its first Mags for study.

5 APRIL 2118, 2000 HOURS
CHEYENNE MOUNTAIN
COLORADO SPRINGS, CO

Simon Ward was informed that President Holcomb was in his quarters with his wife and two children. He directed the Head of the President's Secret Service Detail to inform Holcomb that he needed to speak with The Boss, now. I'll be in the Presidential Briefing Room.

"Yes, sir," said Arlen Winthrop, I'll speak with him now."

Once he arrived in the Briefing Room, Simon placed a call to General Hank Morse and suggested that he might want to attend the meeting with Holcomb.

Morse was in his office when the call came through. He agreed and immediately made his way to the Briefing Room.

There was a computer tech available twenty-four-seven for just these quick meetings. The COS directed him to display the fastest route from Moundsville, West Virginia to Atlanta.

He also directed the Duty Officer to contact Fort Benning to prepare sufficient helicopters to comfortably transport seven people to the CDC.

As the three most powerful men in the world entered the room, they shook hands before seating themselves at the end of the table closest to the wall-mounted one-hundred-inch computer screen.

Both the President and General Morse immediately recognized the highlighted route from Moundsville to Atlanta.

The COS then briefed the two men on the telephone conversation with Doctor Deen at the CDC. He did, however, leave out the discussion on Presidential Directives. When he completed his briefing the President turned to General Morse and asked, "Hank, do you think we can intercept this Professor Abraham and his team? The quicker we get that data to Deen, well, I'm sure you understand the need for speed."

"Yes, sir," said Morse, "I don't think we'll see much traffic on the roads right now, so, yes, sir, I think we have a good chance of an interception." He then picked up the phone to the Duty Officer (DO) and directed him to get the Benning Air Ops on the line.

The connection was immediate as Benning was standing by for orders. Following the General's guidance, Hank placed a call to Colonel Tom Merritt.

"Colonel Merritt, sir, how may I be of assistance to the Chairman of the Joint Chiefs?"

"Tom, before I tell you what I have for you, President Holcomb has a message. Are you sitting down?" smiled General Morse.

"Yes, sir, of course, please put him through."

"General Merritt?" said the President with a grin.

"Yes, sir, but it's Colonel, not General."

"Tom, are you suggesting that I don't know to whom I am speaking? I said, General because as of this moment you are promoted to the rank of Major General."

Tom was thunderstruck with the news. He said, "Mr. President, I, I don't know what to say, er, thank you, sir."

"General, I am truly sorry that your promotion could not be made into a grand affair, but I'm sure you understand that things are a bit in flux right now. I suggest you go to the PX and get some two-star pins. Congratulations General, you are now, to the best of our knowledge the highest-ranking officer on the surface. Here's General Morse."

"Congrats, Tom, I am extremely pleased to say that there is no one better qualified for the job, either now, or before the collapse. Now, here is what is happening tonight…" said Morse as he briefed his new General on the current air mission.

Tom said, "Sir, thank you for the head's up. I'll scoot right over to the flight line and tag along."

"Tom," said General Morse, "are you sure that's such a good idea?"

"Sir, the reason I intend to go is so that there is no mistake in communication. I will retrieve the data, but I will not kidnap this group.

If they want to return to Benning with us, well, that's well and good. If not, I'll wish them well and send them on their way."

"Hmmm, yes, I see the logic of your plan, good idea, go ahead and run with it. Good luck, Tom, you had better get a move on. Out, here."

5 APRIL 2118, 2345 HOURS
FLIGHT LINE (HELICOPTER)
FORT BENNING, GEORGIA

General Merritt arrived at the Helo Flight Line at 2125, still wearing his Colonel's pins, he found a twin bladed heavy lifter Chinook CH47P, and two Cobra VII-J Gunships prepared to lift-off. The Ch47P model had been in service for ten years and in its final iteration was eighty-two feet long and twenty-two feet wide. The lift capacity had been increased from eighty-thousand pounds to one-hundred and thirty-five thousand pounds. The range had also been increased from eight-hundred miles to twelve-hundred, at a cruising speed of two-hundred and eighty miles per hour at an altitude of thirty-five thousand feet. The origins of this magnificent helicopter traced its ancestry back to 1957.

The Cobra Gunships were also too good to remain in the rubbish bin of history, when in 2035, this narrow profile dominator of the fluid battlefield was resurrected, upgraded and placed back into service. The top speed of the Super Cobra VII-D was in excess of five hundred miles per hour with a range of eight-hundred miles.

General Merritt delayed the lift-off until 2400 hours to give the Moundsville convoy time to get well within the range of his helicopter's search fan.

The Rangers, who typically are at the pointy end of the spear, took the delay in stride and began sleeping, reading, or playing poker.

At 2345 Tom ordered the Helicopter Drivers to wind 'em up. He climbed aboard the Shnook and made his way to the pilots to let them know he was onboard and ready to begin the search. On board the Chinook the squad of Rangers quickly began rechecking their equipment. Those soldiers, who know their way around bullet launchers, do not take anything for granted. There was also a ground crew aboard to provide refueling and emergency maintenance that might be required on the mission.

Staff Sergeant Malone greeted General Merritt when he returned from the cockpit and found a seat. "Sir, welcome aboard, my name is Sergeant Malone, and I am in command of the security detail. Do you have any mission updates for me, sir?"

"It is good to meet you, Sergeant. I am happy to see your squad aboard and ready for any possible encounter with Mags or Bad Boys, and no, I have no updates. I'm just along for the ride and to make sure the package gets delivered to the CDC. Sergeant Malone, have you had any deployments to the Sandbox?"

"Yes, sir, three. My first as a Private and I just returned from my third as a Squad Leader."

"Good, good, I'm happy to know that we have some useful experience along for this ride."

As the engines began to wind up, Sergeant Malone said, "Yes, sir, if you'll excuse me, I'll get buckled in."

General Merritt then donned his helmet so he could remain aware of situational updates.

5 APRIL 2118, 2000
ARMORY MAIN ENTRANCE
MOUNDSVILLE, WV

Jake's four-vehicle convoy, consisted of two M-27 carry-alls, with trailers, and two lightly armored M-273A4 Reconnaissance Vehicles. The second M-273A4 trailered a 500-gallon fuel bladder.

In the hours before departure, four members of the team began loading weapons, personal gear, and rations, while the remaining personnel provided security.

The First Sergeant had cleaned out his home weapons safe and loaded four M-86A2 Infantry Assault rifles, four handguns, and ten thousand rounds of ammunition for each. The ammunition was certainly appreciated as this gave ammo to every member of the team for the weapons garnered from the Armory's Weapons Locker.

During the hour when dusk began to bring on the night, First Sergeant Sanders gave rudimentary instruction on the operation of the military vehicles. It was certainly insufficient to make the drivers fully qualified, but they would be able to keep them on the road.

The convoy departed at 2000 hours when it pulled out onto 9th Street. They crossed the Korean War Veteran's Bridge and crossed from West

Virginia to Ohio. Reentering West Virginia at WV807, the convoy continued to I-77 south toward Atlanta and the CDC.

All went well for the first five hours, but the monotony from long hours resulted in Driver Eddie Pritt to become drowsy, making him far less alert. His vehicle blew a tire just north of Galax, Virginia causing the vehicle to swerve hard to the right and into a concrete abutment which sent the vehicle back across the road and into the highway dividing ditch, where it rolled over a couple of times.

The crash of the number two vehicle caused the column to halt in the middle of I-77 south. The Interstate Highway was wide open with no other traffic. While Jake ran to check on Eddie and Gwen, the First Sergeant grabbed Jake and told him to take Frank to secure the left side of the road while Izzy and Ibrahim secured the right side. The crash led to the death of Eddie and his passenger, Gwen Langstrom.

Because of the lessened situational awareness, no one had spotted the narrow strip of rubber with protruding spikes placed on the road to catch the right front tire of wide vehicles.

Jake had just reached the crash site when weapons fire erupted from the wooded area on the road's right side. The first volley caught everyone by surprise but caught Ibrahim Shah squarely in the chest. Sanders kept running at an oblique angle away from the incoming fire and managed to make it to the drainage ditch just before the wooded area. Catching his breath, he slowly began inching his way into the trees and around the left flank of the shooters and into their rear.

The ambushers maintained a relatively steady rate of fire, which helped Sanders locate the positions of the three shooters. Using the thermal sight on his silenced Assault Rifle, he aimed and fired at the man on the left side of the three-man team. He then took out the man on the right side of the enemy line. This left only the center shooter who quickly realized that his two allies had stopped firing. He shouted to them to discover why they had ceased fire. He soon realized that he was now alone and made an attempt to retreat to safety. His path took him directly to First Sergeant Sanders who shot him in the right shoulder. The impact of the bullet caused the rifle to fly away and knocked the attacker to the ground.

Sanders told the man not to reach for another weapon if he wanted to live for even one more minute.

"I surrender, don't shoot!" shouted the painfully injured man, "Please help me!"

Sanders slowly approached the man, and using his night-vision monocle, saw that this murderous piece of crap had no other weapon in his hand. The ambusher continued to scream in pain, pleading for help.

"Shut up, asshole, eat the pain," said Sanders in a stern authoritative voice.

"Oh, God it hurts."

"Yeah, yeah, I'm really sorry about that. Say, are you sorry about the man you just murdered? Just askin'."

"Oh, yes, I swear I wasn't the one that shot him. I purposely aimed all of my shots high so that I wouldn't hit anyone, I swear to God."

"You do know you're in some deep stuff here, right? Now, tell me, old buddy, are you a member of any gang or group in the area?"

"No, it was just the three of us." He again screamed in pain and pleaded with Sanders to help him.

"We'll see, but first you have to answer my questions, so quit screaming like some ten-year-old little girl. Do you live around here? Oh, wow!" said a surprised Sanders as he looked closely at the man's face. I see you have a teardrop tat under your eye. What's that mean?"

"Oh, that, I just had it put on to show the guards that I was sad about being on a road gang and that I wanted to go straight."

"Really?" said a disbelieving Sanders. "Tell me, dipstick, do you want to feel even more pain? That tat means you murdered a fellow inmate." He then placed the muzzle end of his rifle lightly against the open wound, for emphasis.

"No! Please, stop. Okay, okay, the Warden from the prison freed all inmates yesterday because he couldn't feed us no longer. Sides, they was only the three of us prisoners left."

"Thanks, oh, by the way, what's your name?"

The pain had begun to ease somewhat as the man slipped deeper into shock and blood loss. He now knew that he would get no help from this man. He raised his middle finger in defiance and said, "Pliskin, Snake Pliskin."

"Yeah, sure it is, okay, have it your way, Mr. Snake Pliskin." Sanders stood and taking a step back, shot Pliskin in the chest.

6 APRIL 2118, 0200
1000 FT ABOVE I-77

GALAX, VIRGINIA

Over the helmet's intercom connection, Merritt heard, "Colonel, please come up to the flight deck, we are seeing gunfire on I-77."

"Roger," said Merritt, as he broke the connection and made his way to the pilots where he again plugged in his helmet.

The Co-pilot pointed the flashes out to Merritt and asked, "Sir, how should we proceed?"

"Connect me to the Cobras."

"Yes, sir."

General Merritt said, "Cobra 6, this is Ranger 6, scoot on down to the OK Corral and check on the shoot-out. Remain cocked, but not locked. Repeat, you are not cleared to open fire unless fired upon. Just check it out."

"Roger 6," said Cobra 6. "Understand cocked, not cleared to fire unless fired upon, observation only." One second later the two Cobras did a yank and bank toward the shooting which culminated with one final shot while the Cobras were still a mile away.

"Ranger 6, Cobra 6, the firing has stopped, and we see three, no, make that four Military Vehicles. Vehicle four has crashed. People on the ground are coming out from apparent defensive positions and are waving at us. There is one body on the ground. Request permission to land to offer assistance."

"Roger, but first use your speaker to demand they lay down any weapons. Cobra five to provide overt cover."

The pilot of Cobra 6 landed his chopper roughly fifty feet from the personnel who had laid down their weapons and moved away from them. The pilot exited his ship and ordered the Gunner/Co-pilot to remain on board with weapons at the ready.

Jake and First Sergeant Sanders, with raised hands, approached the pilot at a brisk pace. After quick introductions, the pilot returned to his Cobra and directed the Gunner to contact Ranger 6 with the all clear, and friendlies down.

6 APRIL 2118
WALMART
PRESCOTT, AZ

DJ Foote sat behind his mic and continued to alert survivors of the formation of the Prescott Militia. He gave the location and asked for recruits.

"Prescottonians, the Prescott Militia has been formed by Colonel C. Sharpe and Captain Jim Mason. The goal is to grow our force by assigning groups, led by veterans to occupy other large stores like Walmart, Costco, etc. As we occupy these sources of survival needs, food, water, weapons, and ammunition, we will be able to take the fight to the monsters who now roam our streets seeking to kill us. You need not be a veteran to join up, but trained veterans will provide the basic cadre of leadership. Join us in taking back our town. It is ours, and we will not cede it to savages. Bring weapons, ammo, food, and water if you have them."

Within hours of the broadcasts by DJ Foote began showing results as others wanting to join the Prescott Militia began arriving at the Walmart. Most of the recruits were veterans, of all ages, well, up to about sixty. There didn't seem to be anyone older than that, or younger than ten or so.

Upon hearing DJ's broadcast, Jim Mason took Colonel Sharpe aside and said, "Captain? You told him I'm a Captain? No disrespect intended here, Colonel, but are you crazy? I'm a grunt, not no officer."

"Oh, Jimmy, don't be such a wuss, you know enough, hell, I guarantee you know more than some butter-bar Second Looie. You've seen Captains work. Now, if you listen, I will give you some wonderful advice that will guarantee your success. First, the thirteenth rule of leadership, when in charge, take charge. Secondly, and just as important as the first is to listen and learn from the senior NCOs that I'll make sure can guide you. Simple, right?"

"Well," said a not totally convinced Captain Mason, "if you really think that I can pull it off."

Colonel Sharpe gave Jim a firm look and said, "Listen, Captain, if I didn't think you could pull it off, you would not be a Captain. Since we met, I know, it was only yesterday, you have shown me a maturity and a good mind. That will get you through for now, okay?"

"Well, okay, thanks for the vote of confidence."

By 1600 hours of 6 April 2118, the Prescott Militia had grown to twenty-five. Most of the recruits were vets, and more importantly, most were NCOs with experience in using bullet launchers. Things were shaping up.

Recently retired Sergeant First Class Warren Powell was promoted to First Sergeant. He immediately began organizing the recruits into fire teams. Platoons and Squads would come as the organization grew.

First Sergeant Powell requested permission to occupy and requisition the items in the three local Army Supply Stores.

"Good thinking, Sergeant, go ahead and make it happen."

6 APRIL 2118
WORLD SITUATION

Humanity may be one the edge of extinction elsewhere in the world, but countries like the U.S. Israel, and Switzerland were, for the most part, holding their own.

Small and medium towns and communities across America began to group themselves in militias both large and small. They took control of those items needed for survival and then began the retaking of their country.

Large cities, however, did not fare so well, as far too many of the survivors were gang-bangers who fought the Mags and other gangs. By the time it became apparent that these city dwellers could not work together, it was too late.

6 APRIL 2118
TEMECULA, CA

Trent Allison had spent the last several days sitting on the veranda of the resort, reading, drinking wine and sitting in the perfect Spring temperatures. His one lament was that while he had a nice grill and an excellent generator, he discovered, upon opening the Resort's Freezer, that all of the meats had thawed and spoiled. Finally, Trent settled for a can of ham which he grilled to perfection.

He had no inkling of the Hiding Time, as it came to be called. He remained most pleased with himself as he whiled away the hours on the best vacation of his life. Paradise, however, can also become a bore, and so it was for Trent. He thought that perhaps he would make his way to San Diego. He had family there, and with a bit of luck, they may still be alive.

Trent had become somewhat uneasy over the last several hours. He was unable to put his finger on exactly what had set him a bit on edge. He finally wrote it off to getting on the road to Diego.

He stood and laid the book he had been reading, "The Short Happy Life of Francis Macomber," on the side table.

As Trent made his way back to his suite, he thought of Macomber, who had been a rich man married to a beautiful, yet unfaithful, shrew of a woman who took great pleasure in tormenting and humiliating him in front of other people. This witch also made no real secret of her many affairs with other men.

While on safari in Kenya, MacComber finds the rebirth of his self-worth. He announced his decision to divorce this constant burr under his saddle upon their return to America. Francis felt better, more self-confident, and more manly than he had for many years.

Word came by messenger that a man-eating lion was killing the natives of a nearby village. Francis decided to volunteer to go along and take the first shot to bring down the lion.

In the final chapter, he is standing bravely before the lion with his rifle raised to fire. Both the White Hunter and Mrs. MacComber were behind Francis to provide covering fire if he missed. As he squeezed the trigger, a shot rang out, striking Francis in the back of the head. The Hunter then fired and killed the lion. Mrs. MacComber claims that her shot, which killed her husband, was an accident. Mr. Francis MacComber did indeed have a short, happy life.

As Trent returned to his luxurious suite, he made a turn to his right and found himself face to face with a monster. He had no chance to run or draw his weapon before a club struck him just above his nose.

The Mag was dressed in a Policeman's dirty, ragged uniform. As this creature looked down at Trent's body, a glint of sunlight struck a shiny, metal nametag which read, Jones.

7 APRIL 2118, 0200
I-77, GALAX, VA

Once cleared, the Chinook also landed. The Rangers quickly exited the craft and set up a defensive perimeter. General Merritt exited the chopper after Sergeant Malone gave the all clear.

Jake, First Sergeant Sanders, and the remnants of the Dig Team were introduced to General Merritt, who then explained why a Major General was wearing the Eagle collar pins of a Full Bird Colonel. Turning to First Sergeant Sanders, Merritt asked, "Top, are you in charge of this group?"

"No, sir, I came along in the hope of finding an Army Unit in need of a First Sergeant. I was the Top Sergeant for the Virginia National Guard's Bravo Company, 219th Airborne, sistered up with the 18th Airborne Corps at Benning."

"Any combat jumps, Top?"

"Yes, sir, two in Colombia and three in Berzerkistan. Our Company has made seven deployments in the last twelve years. I was a Staff Sergeant back then. In two of our deployments, we were utilized as Straight Leg Infantry."

"Impressive resume, Top, but I don't currently have a billet for a First Sergeant. Would you consider a promotion to Command Sergeant Major, working directly for me?" chuckled General Merritt.

Upon hearing that the General had no billet for him, turned Izzy's smile into a frown, until he heard the General's offer. Now, an enormous smile lit his face, and for the first time in a week, his eyes became bright.

"Oh, hell yes, er, I mean, yes sir, I would like that."

"Good man, now please go find Sergeant Malone for an introduction and situation report (SitRep). Welcome aboard," said Merritt as he reached out to shake the hand of his new Command Sergeant Major into the command.

Jake interrupted and asked about the bodies of his team.

Sergeant Major Sanders said, "Excuse me, General, I was also planning on directing Sergeant Malone to secure the bodies from the wrecked vehicle. We'll transport them back to Benning for burial."

"Good plan, see to it," answered the General.

"Hey, Top, er, I mean, Sergeant Major, what about the other bodies?" asked Jake.

Sanders simply said, in a way that left no question as to his meaning, "What other bodies?"

Merritt then shook hands with Jake and said, "Professor, you have become quite famous in the last few hours. I just spoke with President Holcomb. He asked me to make sure that I met with you and request that you come to Fort Benning for briefings and conversations with the President."

Jakes cautious radar flared on his mind's screen as he said, "General, I didn't know that the VPOTUS was now the President. What happened?"

Tom's face sagged just a bit, as he said, "The President's bunker at Mount Weather was exposed to the Mag-Flu for only seconds, and that was enough. President Greene became ill and turned. There were few survivors. Vice-President Holcomb was in the Cheyenne Mountain Facility and was sworn in as President. He's a good man, Professor Abraham and I think he just might be the man."

"General," said Jake, "I'm not sure I want to be placed in a situation that I can't get out of. It's not that I don't trust you, no, wait a second, I guess, since I don't know you, well, no, I don't fully trust you. Looking around I realize that you have the manpower to force us to go with you, but if you do that, you will never know if what I tell you is true, or just lies because I'd be pissed off."

Tom Merritt laughed before saying, "Well, sir, I guess I understand your position, but a couple of your assertions are inaccurate. Primarily, the President has ordered that no one is to be forced into servitude or held against their will. If you come to Benning, you come of your own volition.

"If you wish to continue on as you are, there are two things I will do. Number one is to relieve you of the data on the Mags so the material can get to the CDC as quickly as possible. The second thing is that, since you are down to only four in your little group, I will allow you to keep two of these borrowed U.S. Army vehicles and if you are short of ammunition, we will give you what we have with us. I know that NG Armories don't normally have ammunition on-site. I wish I could offer more, but that is about all we have here. Is this acceptable to you?"

"General Merritt," said a thankful, though still somewhat skeptical Jacob Abraham, "I will pass on your offer and ask if any of my people wish to go with you."

Tom smiled and said, "Fair enough, but would you mind making a video recording of our meeting, along with your concerns; anything you think might be of use to the President?"

"Of course, I'll get right on it and have it ready by the time you have the extra vehicle loaded on the CH47. If you'll excuse me, General, I'd like to speak with my crew now."

"Of course," replied Tom, "you know where to find me when you are ready."

Jake turned to the remaining three members of the original Dig Team. Getting right to the point, Jake said, "Well, my friends, we have come to a potential crossroads. General Merritt will take the data and get it to the CDC. He has also offered to take us to Fort Benning for some debriefings for President Holcomb. Apparently, President Greene died of the Mag-Flu.

"I told him that I did not intend to go with him at this time. I expected him to object and insist that we accompany him. He surprised me when he said that we were free to go. He also promised ammunition for the Machine Guns and said we could keep two of the vehicles. So, okay, I need to know what you would like to do."

Sarah spoke up first saying, "Professor Abraham, I hope you will understand, but I want to go to the CDC. Always looking over my shoulder for monsters is not for me, so I'll take the relative safety option."

Frank also apologized and said, "Sir, I think I'd like to go with the General and re-up."

Jake gave them his blessing and directed them to the General. This left only Jake and Gale. Looking at Gale, Jake asked, "Well, Gale, what is your preference?"

"Jake, my love, I'll go anywhere with you, you know that but how safe can we be on our own, I mean, just the two of us?"

He looked at Gale and said, "Yes, I know you're right, but I am loathe to trust anyone in the government, especially at a time like this, but yeah, we can't afford to be unrealistic. Come on, let's go tell the Generalissimo that we will go with him."

CHAPTER SEVEN

6 APRIL 2118, 0910
HEADQUARTERS, 175TH RANGER REGIMENT,
FORT BENNING, GA

Command Sergeant Major Israel Sanders greeted Jake and Gale as they entered the General's outer office. "Jake, I didn't get a chance to say this at the ambush site; I want you to know how happy I am that you accepted the General's invitation."

"Hi, Iz, it's good to see you, too. Is the General in, we have an appointment."

"Yes and no," smiled the Command Sergeant Major, he's over in the Post Headquarters building in the Commo Room. He'll meet both y'all there."

"All right, but why there?" asked Jake.

"Well, you two being celebrities and all, President Holcomb is anxious to meet up with you."

"Yeah, well, I guess I should have expected as much. Okay, are you coming?

Before Iz could answer, Gale interrupted, saying, "Whoa, wait just one damned minute. I can't meet the President looking like this. Come on, Jake, I look like a refugee. No way, uh huh, I have to fix my hair and get some decent clothes. He'll just have to wait."

Jake and Izzy laughed at the idea of making the President of the United States wait so Gale could fix her hair. "Come on, Gale, you look scrumptious, but even if you didn't, we still can't keep The Man waiting, so come on, let's go."

Now Gale's eyes became those of a deer in the headlights as she said, "Oh, Jacob, I look like a schlemiel."

Izzy chimed in with, "Gale, he's right, you look fantastic, and what is a schlemiel?"

Now Gale began to regain her sense of humor, "Izzy, a schlemiel is someone who looks like a bum or a klutz, and right now that defines me. Come on, Jake, do I really have to go now?"

"Ayup," said Jake as they got into the Command Sergeant Major's carryall.

"Oh, all right, but you both know that you are gonna pay for my embarrassment, right?"

"Come on, hon…"

"Oh no, don't you honey me," but the corners of her mouth betrayed the hint of a smile.

Seven minutes later, Jacob, Gale, and Izzy, were ushered into the large Conference Room by the General's Aide, Captain Mark Meadows.

As the three entered the room, Tom raised his head from his tablet containing briefing notes. He smiled when he saw his new friends and said, "Jake, Gale, Sergeant Major Sanders, it's good to see you. I must say that your timing is impeccable; the meeting with the President and his Staff starts in ten minutes. I know everyone was certainly tired and stressed out last night, so I think we should go over the events of the ambush one more time. Ladies first, Gale, if you would please tell us your experience in the ambush."

"Oh, sure," said Gale, "well, let's see, I was driving while Jake was looking over a road map of Atlanta to get to the CDC. Damned truck had no GPS. We were in the number three position, right behind the vehicle that blew a tire. When it went, I mean it went flat fast. The tire seemed to disintegrate in the first few feet or so.

"I saw Eddie try to recover, but the vehicle was beyond that ever happening. It veered into a concrete abutment on the right which sent it veering back to the left and into the median. Once it went there, the vehicle began to roll two times. I'd guess that Eddie and Gwen were killed almost at once. At that point, I was stopped, so I jumped from the carry-all and ran down into the ditch to see if I could help Eddie or Gwen.

"The gunfire began just as I reached the edge of the ditch. I don't really know more than that because while the others were engaging the shooters, I kept trying to get to my friends.

"General, that pretty much sums up my portion of the incident. Though, I must say that I find it awfully coincidental that there were shooters right where Frank's tire blew. Did they shoot the tire?"

General Merritt said, "thank you, Gale, good report, and no, we found a nail-filled board still stuck to a part of the tire. You definitely ran into an ambush."

Turning to Jake, Merritt said, "Jake, tell us what happened from your perspective."

"Yes, sir, sure, the Sergeant Major and I came together at the top of the ditch, but when the firing started Izzy told me to take Frank and secure the left side of the roadway. At that time, we didn't know that the shooters were only on the right side. In hindsight, it seems to me that those bastards didn't have a clue about how to set up a crossfire ambush, and actually, I'm very happy about that.

"Frank and I took up covered positions on the far side of the ditch and basically just set up a small blocking position. It was the Sergeant Major who took off toward the shooters. Unfortunately, as they ran across the road, obliquely from the rifle fire, Ibrahim took two rounds squarely in the chest.

"Sir, I don't really know the details of what happened next, but I do know that if Iz hadn't flanked the ambushers, well, we might all be dead. All I know for sure is that he took out all three of those murderous bastards, all by himself."

"Thank you, Jake," said Merritt, and turning to his new Command Sergeant Major, Merritt said, "So, Izzy, is it? Apparently, you neglected to fully detail your contribution to this little firefight. I think you should be a bit more forthcoming and tell us exactly what you did, and don't you dare give me any, aw-shucks humble pie, hit wuzn't nuthin, crap. Come on, out with it."

Sanders was caught off guard from his General's tone and said, "Yes, sir, well, um, sir, I just did what my training told me to do. I made it to the wood line on the enemies left flank, then I crept up behind them. The dumbasses had no rear security, at all. So, the first thing I did was to take out the one on the left and then that other dirtball on my right. Using my silenced rifle, the asshat in the middle didn't know what happened to his buddies. Finally, he panicked and tried to run away, which brought him straight to me.

"I wanted some answers, so I shot him in his right shoulder, cause that's the hand he had his piece in. I told him not to reach for any weapon as I approached him. Before he went to hell, he told me that he and two other road gang prisoners had been freed the day before by the Warden. That was when he expired, and I left him there along with the others to rot, hell, sir, the buzzards got to eat same as the worms.

"That was when I heard the gunships coming in, so I went back to the road, laid down my weapon, waved, and smiled my friendliest toothy grin."

General Merritt smiled and said, "Well said, Sergeant Major, colorful, but well said. Bright and early this morning, Frank Lusk came to the Sergeant Major and offered to enlist. He is now back in harness as a Staff Sergeant. Jake, the Sergeant Major tells me that you are also prior service, a grunt, I understand. He also said you came out an E-5 Buck Sergeant. That about right?"

"Yes, sir, I joined up right out of High School for three years in Germany but ended up here at Benning and then in Berzerkistan."

"Um, huh," asked the General, "and is that all, Jake?"

"Well, yes sir, I was just your normal, ordinary straight leg grunt; did my three years, then went to college on my GI Bill at the University of Charleston. I took my Master's from the West Virginia College of Graduate Studies and finished up my Ph.D. at West Virginia University. Following that, I was hired on as a Teaching Professor in Paleontology, and later I added Archaeology. Beyond that, sir, I don't know what else to add."

"Oh, really," said Merritt, "didn't you leave out that little part about a Bronze Star, Silver Star, Combat Infantry Badge, and a Purple Heart?"

Talking about his exploits in combat always embarrassed Jake, and he responded by saying, "Well, yes sir, there is that, but really, both incidents were blown way out of proportion. I just happened to be at the wrong place at the right time, not to mention the fact that I was also damned lucky enough to get out alive."

Merritt looked at Sanders and said, "There, Iz, you see what I mean with that humble pie crap. Let me tell you what his record says. While on patrol his squad was ambushed, two men immediately went down with serious injuries. One of those men was the Radioman. Now guess who ran out into live enemy fire to retrieve, not only the Radioman but the wounded Squad Leader. In the process, young Sergeant Abraham took a through and through round just below his liver. He then established firing points in an attempt to hold out until help could arrive.

"Let's not forget that he had a through and through wound just below the liver. Did he lay down and demand the Squad Medic see to his wound? Nope, he took command of the situation because the Squad Leader was unconscious from a head wound. The only medical assistance he received was the packing of his wounds with clotting cloth to stop his bleeding. Sergeant Abraham's leadership and poise while under attack saved the lives of every man on that patrol, by keeping the enemy at bay for ten minutes until the gunships arrived to clear the area for the Reaction Force.

"Personally, I think he should have received the Medal of Honor, but that's neither here nor there. Professor Jacob Abraham, the saying is once a Sheep Dog, always a Sheep Dog, congratulations, Jake, you have just been recalled to active duty with the rank of Captain."

Gale dragged Jake into the hallway and said, "What? Just say no, or even hell no, I won't go. Burn your draft card, whatever."

"Gale, this is still the United States of America, and the oath I took wasn't voided when I finished my three-year hitch. Gale, my sweet, if I don't go, I'll be a deserter, and if I get caught, they'll probably send me to the CDC as a guinea pig. Besides, we might be able to be of some use."

"We?" asked Gale.

"Hey, if I have to go, I'd like you with me."

"I don't know," said Gale, "I love you, but…"

"Come on, Bubbala (Boo-buh-luh), we'll be together and, besides, where would you go, and what would you do? Don't forget that it was you who said that we wouldn't be safe with just the three of us."

"Yeah," said Gale, "there is that. Oh, what the hell, I guess I'm in if you think it's best. But, Jake, what will I be, a Private? Wait a minute, what do you mean by just the three of us?" asked a confused Gale.

Jake laughed and said, "You, me, and Russell, of course."

Both laughed as they got ready for the President's meeting. Gale had forgotten all about her hair. As they walked back into the Conference Room, Gale elbowed Jake and whispered, "Bubbala? You always seem to slip in some Yiddish when you want to soft-soap me. You could have just said something like Darling, you know."

"Yes, I could have, but I like the sound of my little Bubbala better."

The Cheyenne Mountain Presidential Conference Room came online at 1000 hours. Introductions were made all around, then Jake, Gale, and Izzy, all had to again go over their stories of the ambush. As a courtesy, the President also asked about the Dig site and the Team. Jake began his tale from the beginning and ended with the ambush. The only thing he left out was the Walmart incident involving Frank.

The President and his Staff listened intently to Jake's story. Holcomb finally said, "Captain Abraham, I just want to personally thank you for the data you provided the CDC. Your team member, sorry, I forget her name, oh, wait, yes, Sarah, yes, that's it, seems very happy to be there. I have instructed Dr. Deen to offer her an AI that will be connected to your commo section. In this way, she can keep you up to date, and informed about her duties there. I just thought you might want to keep in minimal touch, at least. Captain Abraham, General Morse and I have discussed your mission with General Merritt. He will go over it with you following this meeting. I hope you haven't forgotten your sneaky-Pete experiences in Berzerkistan."

Jake's eyes darted to Merritt who just smiled back at him.

Following the video meeting with Cheyenne Mountain, Jake, Gale, and Russell, who laid at Jake's feet, sat down with General Merritt. The General was just a bit concerned about Gale being in the meeting, and he asked Jake if her presence was necessary.

Before Gale could get out of her seat to leave, in a huff, Jake looked into the General's eyes and said, "General Merritt, Gale Storm holds a Ph.D. in Paleontology which will be of imminent importance in our fight against these Mags. She is my partner, she is disciplined, good with firearms, and not afraid of anything, so please, let's get her role sorted out right away, sir.

I accept that you can call me back to active duty, but I also request that because of her specialized training and education, she certainly meets current Medical Corps requirements to be given a direct commission to First Lieutenant. Please understand, sir that I am not making any demands, here, I am simply pleading a case to request your special consideration for commissioning, sir."

General Merritt leaned back in his chair and smiled at both Jake and Gale. He said, "Captain, that was an eloquent and passionate plea to commission Miss Gale Storm. In the last few days, I have commissioned many an enlisted man to the Officer Corps with far fewer credentials than Gale. The President and General Morse have given broad powers to me in such matters. First Lieutenant Storm, welcome to the United States Army. Jake, may I assume that you will teach her the rudimentary courtesies of the military, you know, saluting and such?"

"Yes, sir," said Jake as he turned to Gale saying, "Bubbala, say thank you to the General."

Gale was far more proper in her bearing than Jake. She said, "Thank you, General, I promise to work hard to make you know you have made the right decision, sir."

Merritt then swore both into the Army for a term not to exceed six months beyond the conclusion of the Mag War. Following this ceremony, with the Command Sergeant Major looking on as a witness, all four again sat at the table to hear the plan for Jake's small unit.

"Captain," said the General, "My vision of your unit, name it what you wish, will consist of no less than thirteen personnel. I envision the following:

- Commander
- XO
- Senior NCO, rank E7
- Doctor
- 2 Nurses
- 2 Medics
- 7 Man Security Team
- 1 each E-6, Staff Sergeant
- 6 each E-4 and below

"This, of course, is just a baseline estimate. Should the need arise, we will increase the number of personnel to suit the individual mission. The Command Sergeant Major will work with you to flesh out the personnel. This brings us to your first assignment. Your team will be flown to Atlanta to initiate a database on Mag culture. The CDC also wants a Mag child for study and research."

Jake said, "That's all you want, sir? Now let me get this straight. Basically, you want us to just casually hang out with a Mag Clan, then steal one of their children? I think we should also need to keep in mind that the youngest of their children will be from around eleven to thirteen, right? Well, from what I have gleaned from my study of the Mags, eleven or twelve is an adult."

Merritt smiled at his Command Sergeant Major and said, "See, Sergeant Major, I told you he would catch on right away."

"Oh, yes sir," replied the Sergeant Major, "but, I can't wait to hear how he plans to kidnap a Mag kid."

"Yes, sir," snapped Jake, "How do you propose that we accomplish the snatch?"

The General smiled, shrugged his shoulders and said, "Oh, come on Captain, you'll think of something."

Turning to Gale, Jake said, "Yeah, right, heaven help us, we're in the hands of maniacs."

"Good, now can you think of anything else you might need in the way of equipment?"

"Yes, sir, off-hand I think we'll need a dart gun with anesthesia to knock the kid and any adults with him out cold. I also want each team member to receive an AI linked to our commo, which needs to be added to the team."

"Done. The Sergeant Major will coordinate whatever you need. Oh, I forgot to mention that you are scheduled to depart for Atlanta in three days. Jake, you have carte blanche here, but you also need to have a sense of urgency putting together your team, Roger?"

"Yes, sir, is there anything else I need to know?"

Merritt stood, shook Jake's hand and said, "Captain, your missions may be many and varied. They may take you, well, wherever you are needed. Sergeant Major, please give the good Captain and his XO whatever support he needs. This team is your number one priority for the next three days, Roger?"

"Roger sir," said the Command Sergeant Major.

General Merritt then stood up, signaling that the meeting was over. After shaking hands and wishing Jake well, the Sergeant Major escorted Jake, Gale, and Russell back to his office, where the planning phase of Operation Snatch would begin in earnest.

Back in the Command Sergeant Major's office the equipment list and personnel (TO&E) was fleshed out.

"Iz," said Jake, "the team will also need an XO. If an experienced Officer is unavailable, I have no problem with commissioning a combat proven NCO to a First Lieutenant. In fact, let's go that route and promote a proven NCO."

Gale interrupted saying, "Wait, I thought I was the XO, whatever that is."

"Yes, and that is exactly why I want combat, field experience in that position. You will remain by my side to learn about the military, tactics, and decorum. Gale, I hope you don't take offense here, but I need someone who has been in real combat in our leadership positions. As you gain that experience, your duties and responsibilities will increase, okay?"

"Yeah, when I think about it, I realize that's the right path to follow. Okay, sir, make a leader out of me."

"LT," said a serious Captain Abraham, "you are already a leader, I have to turn you into a soldier. If I didn't think you were that leader, I would never have asked for your commissioning."

7 APRIL 2118
CAIRO, EGYPT

Cairo, much like every country in the world that failed to allow firearms to be owned by their citizens became bleeding grounds as the Mags decimated the unarmed populace. By the time Humans managed to group themselves into defensive perimeters, the battle for supremacy was already lost. The Mags soon came to avoid these defenses until those Humans either starved or came out to find food and water. Those who came out failed to return.

Cairo was a city of nearly fifty million people before the Mag-Flu struck. This reduced the population by nearly 90%, to roughly six million. The death toll was far above the first world average of a 75% reduction in population. When the Mags appeared, the population was reduced another 50%, to around three million.

The Mags took a terrible toll of Human survivors, and hygienic diseases took the remainder. In less than a month, Egypt and most other countries were under the sole ownership of the Cro-Magnons. Entire ethnic groups just disappeared within weeks of the Mag's appearance.

Throughout the Middle East, only those countries where firearms were readily available were able to stave off the Mag infestation. Israel's population dropped to fifty-thousand when the sick went into hiding. Only discipline, freedom to own firearms, and the Grace of God saved the Jews from extinction.

7 APRIL 2118
SWITZERLAND

Switzerland was the most successful nation in Europe to secure their nation against the Mag attacks. Gun ownership saved this traditionally neutral nation, while the other nations of the European Union began to fall like ten-pins. Ancient fortresses once again resumed the role of defense. The surviving militaries of these nations began a program of arming the populace, which blunted the Mag assault upon Humanity. Still, the populations were so decimated that there could be no stopping the new Dark Age that would spread across Europe, Asia, and East Asia.

7 APRIL 2118
BEIJING, CHINA

Within days of the Mag emergence, the Asian world suffered to the point of near extinction. China was hit especially hard as the military was forbidden to issue weapons to the Chinese people, for fear of a counter-revolution against the ruling Communist State.

Should Mankind survive this Mag War, the world's maps would see dramatic revisions.

9 APRIL 2118
175TH RANGER REGIMENTAL HQ
FORT BENNING, GA

Jakes team had fleshed out well, and the team was set to fly to Atlanta the following day, via Ch47. The plan was to land in front of the CDC to establish, and secure, a small perimeter around the Shnook. From there Captain Abraham, First Lieutenant Storm, and Sergeant Russell would begin the away mission.

Once word got out about the formation of a special team to study the Mag Culture and to carry out missions that would put them at the pointy end of the spear, the Command Sergeant Major had a long list of volunteers. However, due to the nature of the upcoming missions, the recruits volunteering for the Security Section were limited to Rangers only, in the rank of E-7 and below.

Jake would have been happy to have Staff Sergeant Frank Lusk assigned to the team, but he had been given other duties involving the capture and securing of one of the many food distribution centers nearest to Fort Benning.

The Mags in the immediate areas surrounding Fort Benning outnumbered General Merritt's force by several hundred to one, but the Soldiers were supremely confident in their force multiplier; firearms.

10 APRIL 2118 0700
HEADQUARTERS, 175TH RANGER REGIMENT,
FORT BENNING

Staff Sergeant Lusk and his Assistant-Squad Leader sat at General Merritt's Conference Table as the new Division G-3 (Plans and Ops) stood before a computer-generated map of the insertion point for their portion of Operation Trap.

"Sergeant, as you can see, the objective is to insert your force into the Walmart Supercenter located at 385 Callaway Church Rd, Lagrange, GA, which is due north of the Benning Front Gate.

"Sergeant Lusk, your force is the lynchpin of the entire operation. You must take and hold the Walmart position. Your squad has been reinforced with:

- Squad Leader
- Asst. Squad Leader
- 12 Squad Machine Gunners
- 22 Infantrymen/Standard Issue Rifle
- 4 Grenadiers
- 2 each, Medics, Combat
- 12 each, Squad Machine Guns
- 4 each, Auto Launchers, Grenade
- 40 each, Sidearms, 9 mm
- 120,000 each, 7.62 Ball, Linked
- 28,000 each, 7.62 Ball, Loose
- 800 each, Grenades, Auto Launched, 40 mm
- 4,000 each, 9mm Ball, Loose
- Rations to come from Walmart canned goods
- 40 each, sets of Body Armor
- AI for each Squad Member connected to Intranet and Squad Commo Section

- Squad Leader/Asst. Squad Leader AI also connected to Fort Benning Mission Control.

"Staff Sergeant Frank Lusk, your objective is considered pivotal to Operation Snag. You will be choppered in to the parking lot of the Walmart Supercenter. This insertion will begin the data baseline for the creation of a Standard Operating Procedure (SOP). These early movements to contact will:

"Establish the groundwork to find the best and safest ways to secure and defend captured objectives.

"This is deemed a requirement, as each objective will serve as an anchor for each new Operational Mission to attack and eliminate the Mag threat.

"It will also allow a safe transit arena to feed both military and the local civilian populace. The third mission goal is to engage and destroy any Mags encroaching upon your outpost.

"Once an outpost is secured, additional troops will be brought in to begin the mission to search out and destroy any and all Mags in the immediate area.

"Once you have secured your objective, two Battalions of Infantry will arrive via helicopter to begin establishing a line to the south of your position. Two battalions of Infantry will simultaneously exit the Benning Main Gate and push north.

"Once these two pincers meet, they will move west, trapping all Mags between the two battalions and the Chattahoochee River. Upon completion of this mission, we will have established a corridor to allow unfettered movement throughout this entire area of roughly ninety square miles. This operation is named Trap, and it is anticipated to take up to ninety days to complete.

"Hundreds of small drones, capable of detecting infrared heat signatures, will move just ahead of the ground forces. The drones will transmit the location of any living thing larger than a house cat to ground control which will then send forces to eliminate any enemy targets. Human civilians will be sent to the rear where they will receive medical check-ups or aid, as required.

"We will not be using Artillery, Armor, or Gunships as we do not want to destroy buildings or infrastructure.

"This initial campaign is intended to create a Mag-free zone to allow the open movement of men and materiel to provide the systematic elimination of any Mag infestation.

"It has been decided to use Walmart Stores as the origination points of insertion as they are in wide distribution and readily recognizable for planning purposes.

"Success of this Operation will prove the concept, and similar Operations from Forts across the U.S. will commence.

"Staff Sergeant Lusk had no significant questions concerning his portion of Operation Trap. He would attack, destroy any enemy present, secure, and hold his Mission Objective until properly relieved. He chuckled to himself that the briefer could have just said, "Take it and hold it, Soldier."

CHAPTER EIGHT

10 APRIL 2118 0900
TEMP OFFICE, CAPTAIN ABRAHAM
FORT BENNING

Jake's 175th Ranger Regiment's, Special Mag Operations Group (Provisional), or the 175th SMOG was shaping up, but way too slowly. The initial plan was for him to have departed Fort Benning for the CDC in Atlanta on the 9th of April. Unfortunately, several of the key players had either not been available or, as yet, found.

Captain Jake Abraham lamented the fact that the air assets originally slated to fly his unit were unavailable. The aircraft were plentiful, but pilots were now in short supply. This lack of assets meant that SMOG would be forced to increase their Tactical Operation Equipment and personnel to maintain them. Again, the problem was not materiel, but personnel.

Jake looked over the newly authorized equipment and personnel lists and sighed. "Izzy, the size of SMOG is getting out of hand, hell, soon we'll be at company strength, and now the G-3 (Plans and Ops) says we need more Grunts to improve security."

General Merritt's Command Sergeant Major smiled at Jake and said, "Sir, more equipment and support personnel means more Grunts with bullet launchers. We have to protect the equipment and the unit personnel, especially the Med folks."

"Okay, I get that, but the plan to ease in quietly, make the snatch and get out without being spotted is now out the window. Hell, we've got clerks, supply, fuel, maintenance, and I'm sure that isn't all. And, if we are spotted, we will come under attack."

"Yes, sir, that is a reasonable assessment, but please don't forget, the overriding mission is to eliminate the Mag infestation. And from what I see here in your new TO&E, you are going to have the opportunity to contribute to that mission."

"Sergeant Major, I know all that, but we, as the President so eloquently put it, are supposed to be Sneaky Pete's, not front-line Grunts."

Looking just a bit more serious now, Sergeant Major Sanders said, "Sir, you know the exigencies of the Service supersede everything else. So, it comes down to hurry up and wait, be flexible, and accomplish any and all assigned missions. Come on, sir, you know all this."

"Yeah, I know, Izzy, but if we have to hurry up and wait much longer SMOG will become a battalion, and I definitely ain't qualified to run one of those."

"Yes, sir, I understand, and I promise that I am doing the best I can to get you on the road."

"Okay, okay, how much longer?"

Sergeant Major Sanders said, "Hopefully not more than another week. Operation Trap has priority, and that is why you will just have to wait until we can muster up your requirements."

10 APRIL 2118
AMISH COUNTRY
PENNSYLVANIA

Lancaster, Pennsylvania was a beautiful area of farms, peaceful people, and quaint horse-drawn carriages, that is, until the Mags arrived. Many an Amish farmer tried to communicate with these creatures. Having suffered their own losses, and realizing the Mags were once human, these non-violent people tried to meet with them and offer help. The Amish were immediately killed, down to every last living soul. Sling blades quickly became the weapon of choice, replacing the club of the Cro-Magnon Man. An ancient form of the age-old Arms Race had begun.

The Amish, Quakers, and all others who sought peace over protecting themselves and their families were quickly overrun. Their existence would be only a memory; a small footnote in future history texts.

By 2118, nearly 75% of all American households held, at least, one firearm. Unfortunately, only a small percentage of the surviving population heard the President's warning to go armed. Those that did hear and followed this advice held up well against the new invader, but a shortage of ammunition often became the downfall of even the bravest of Human Souls.

Churches overflowed and sadly became killing fields. What seemed to have become lost in Church teachings was one simple and basic fact. God gave Man dominion over all things upon the Earth and was given Free Will to decide his own path. It appears that God, having given this gift of Free Will, left Man to stew in his own juices if he screwed it up.

10 APRIL 2118 0900
FLIGHT LINE (HELICOPTER),
FORT BENNING

Staff Sergeant Lusk's reinforced squad had become a platoon. They mounted the waiting helicopters and were quickly transported to the Walmart Supercenter located at 385 Callaway Church Rd, at Lagrange.

10 APRIL 2118 0900
WALMART SUPERCENTER
LAGRANGE, GA

Two Mags had discovered the Walmart at Lagrange on the second day of their rebirth. Over the next few days, they found others suitable to become Clan members and by 10 April their numbers had grown to nearly two-hundred.

The Cro-Magnon Man was ignorant, meaning uneducated, but they were far from stupid. As a result, they very quickly learned how to open plastic and cardboard containers of meats and such items as cereals.

To Modern Humans, those meats would not have been edible, as their time left in nonworking coolers caused them to spoil, but in the process of becoming Mags, their digestive systems had also morphed into a more adaptive ability, allowing them to eat foods Modern Humans would consider carrion.

As the Mags investigated their new home, two discoveries were made that would become a problem for humanity. They discovered bladed weapons, knives and machetes, along with the bow and arrow. No, Mags were not stupid, they were inventors and thinkers.

These discoveries would soon lead to the necessity for developing language.

The discoverers of both blades and the bow quickly demonstrated their finds. In a very short time, the adaptive Mags became skilled in the use of these wonder weapons. Several Clansmen were sent to instruct other communities in the use of the blade and bow. This new Cro-Magnon creature began a second evolution; the development of a warrior class and the rudimentary introduction of speech.

10 APRIL 2118
PRESIDENT'S OFFICE
CHEYENNE MOUNTAIN

At the President's morning Security Brief President Holcomb was updated on the kick-off of both Operation Snatch and Trap. Holcomb directed that a constant live video stream be broadcast on several computer screens throughout the Cheyenne Mountain Facility to show progress in the Mag War.

10 APRIL 2118
WALMART SUPERCENTER
LAGRANGE, GA

Mag guards posted at each open entrance to the cave rushed to tell their leaders of the giant birds that were landing in the stone field. These huge birds were spitting out those other creatures so similar to themselves.

Immediately Mags with blades and bows took up defensive positions within their cave and waited for an attack.

As the helos disgorged the soldiers from their bellies, Scouts noted that there were dozens of dead Mags littering the area near the front door. A cursory inspection showed that they had been killed by gunfire.

The two point-men slowly approached the main entrance to the Walmart store while the remaining force secured the area surrounding the building. Once the outside areas were secured, the Scouts were directed to enter and begin a search to see if the store held Mags.

After only two steps inside the darkened interior, the Scouts knew that the store was far from empty. The smell of Mag habitation was almost overpowering.

The first two Scouts entering the building were brought under fire by Mag arrows. One Trooper was hit squarely in the chest. Fortunately, his body armor deflected the projectile, though the blow did knock him onto his back. As he rose, he heard his partner scream as he was hit in the thigh by an arrow. Both men opened fire in a sweeping motion which killed most of the defenders, but not before each man suffered two additional wounds via arrows. The first man to enter took a final arrow through his right eye while the second man was again hit in his lower leg.

The invaders were now pushing through the doorway firing as they came. Once the arrows stopped flying the Soldiers began a systematic Search and Destroy mission.

As the attackers moved down the candy aisle one young Private bent over to snag a Snickers Bar. A Mag hiding atop the display case jumped from the top shelf and swung his machete over the bent head of the hungry Private. The Mag was immediately killed by a Corporal who told his partner that he should buy some lottery tickets, well, if there were still such things.

The young Private looked from the dead Mag to his Corporal and said, "Corp, I didn't crap my pants, but only because my sphincter had slammed shut. Thanks, I owe you one."

Two additional Troopers were injured, one by an arrow which grazed his neck with a nonlethal wound, and another suffered a deep gash to his left arm from a deflected machete blow.

Within minutes the dead and wounded were flown back to Benning. The Med-Evacs made two trips.

Unnoticed, were four Mags that were returning from teaching a nearby clan the use of the bow and arrow. They saw the entire assault and then snaked their way back to the nearby clan.

One important thing did not go unnoticed by the Mags, the clubs carried by the attackers, spit fire, thunder, and death. It is true that they were frightened, but they were also curious in the use of these clubs that bellowed death. It took nearly an hour for the store to be fully secured.

The final body count was one-hundred and twenty-three members of the clan, one dead Trooper and three wounded. Though the results presented a tremendous victory, the troopers learned a new respect for the Mag.

No, this fight would not go easy. As the briefings would show, 100% of the Mag Clan was down, the forty U.S. Army attackers had suffered a 10% reduction in combat effective personnel. This was a staggering number that would bring about a differing strategy when entering buildings with possible enemy forces inside.

The added strategy relied not on a new technique, but a very old one. Prior to entry, flash-bang grenades would be thrown to disorient the enemy within. Pride and arrogance had caused the first American military injuries and death. This mistake would not be repeated.

Following the removal and burning of the Mag bodies, the internal cleanup began. This proved to be a very nasty job as a large area was used for Mag body waste. Those men unfortunate enough to be assigned the manure detail wore painter's masks sprayed with perfume.

The remaining Soldiers began barricading and securing the entrances to the store.

Within two hours of the assault, two CH-47 Chinook helicopters arrived with the mission essentials, plus four human replacements.

A Ranger Company was flown in and immediately began securing the buildings surrounding the Walmart store.

A thermal drone picked up the presence of possibly two Mags on the ground floor of a two-story O'Reilly's Auto Parts store. The store was in the same strip mall anchored by the Walmart. Squad Leader, Sergeant Larry Corliss called on Corporal Willie White to lead a four-man fire team into the O'Reilly's to check it out.

Corporal White informed his team that it was their turn in the barrel. He ordered Private Stan Wilkins and Private Orville Henderson to toss a couple of flash-bangs through the open front door. The team knew the drill, flash-bangs, then rush in, kill the shook-up Mags, or rescue survivors.

White led his team cautiously to the entrance of the parts store. Everyone on the team was very happy that no arrows came flying at them. After Wilkins and Henderson opened the door, both men tossed in the stun grenades then braced themselves against the walls. They shut their eyes and covered their ears until the grenades detonated. Each man then grabbed a door handle and pulled it open. The remaining two men of the fire team then charged into the storefront.

Two Mags were found writhing on the floor from the effects of the flash-bangs. They were quickly sent straight to hell. Each man was glad they had a painter's mask on, because feces and urine smell seemed to always accompany any Mag wearing pants. It became obvious that the buttons and zippers were beyond the Mags ability to manipulate. Though everyone knew that this would change quickly, even if they had to tear off their ragged clothes. The Rangers figured that pants could only hold so much feces.

The four men continued to clear the building, and when Wilkins and Henderson climbed the stairs, they saw eight dead mags in the hallway leading to the office. The office door had been knocked off its hinges.

"Corp," said Wilkins into his squad radio, you'd better get up here. There's dead Mags all over the place."

"Roger, on the way."

Stepping over the bodies, Henderson entered the store's office. His nose was assaulted by that other nausea causing odor, that of decaying human flesh. Two more dead Mags lay directly in front of the dead man. He had been attacked by Mags carrying machetes and was literally cut into pieces. On the ground next to the body was a book. He picked it up and discovered that the book was a diary that began on the 5th of April and ended on the 8th.

"Hey, Corp," shouted Wilkins, "where are you? I found a diary that the Old Man will want to see."

Among the gore, a .45 caliber pistol was found, but the only sign of a rifle were empty boxes of 7.62 ammo. When Henderson cleared the pistol, he found that the weapon was empty. It seemed pretty obvious that the two dead Mags in front of the man had eaten the last two rounds from the .45.

White and Wilkins met at the office door where the diary and pistol were passed to White.

"Hey, Sarge," said White into his Squad radio. "The store is clear. Wilkins found a diary that should probably be sent up the chain to the Captain."

"Roger, Corporal, hang on to them, we'll meet up with you in about two minutes, Rodriguez and his crew just finished up rescuing two survivors."

"Good deal," replied White, "see ya' in two."

The diary was then passed up the line until it finally reached General Merritt.

"General," said, Lt Colonel Brad Pierce, the Battalion Commander of the team who found the book, "this morning a fire team in the Walmart Plaza came across a diary. I think you should read it, sir. It only covers three days, but, well, you'll see."

"Thank you, Brad, is it important enough to read right now?"

"Yes, sir, it is. That's why I brought it to you personally."

Lt Colonel Pierce returned to his battalion, and General Merritt began reading about the final three days of a man killed by Mags.

5 April to 8 April 2118

From the diary of William Bell

April 5, 2118. I awoke this morning to the sound of a woman screaming. The sounds came from the street just in front of my home. After jumping out of bed and throwing on a pair of jeans, I reached into the drawer beside my bed and grabbed my pistol. Then, rushing barefoot down the stairs to the front room window, I saw a monster standing over a woman. She lay unmoving on the wet concrete. The monster had just hit her with an aluminum baseball bat. Without thinking things through I opened the door and rushed outside to try to help the downed woman.

I screamed at the monster… I know… what was I thinking, right? Anyway, I just blindly reacted. I guess it's true, once a Marine, always a Marine, and time doesn't change that- Semper Fi.

The damned thing turned toward me and howled, then raised the bat, and with amazing speed, it charged across my now weed infested lawn. Again, without thinking, I just instinctively raised my hand and fired. The pistol rocked back in my hand, momentarily obscuring my vision of this demented thing. It was so close that the seventeen inches of flame from the barrel scorched his face. The .45 caliber round had entered the chest, of whatever this thing was. It lay writhing on the ground, still alive. As I looked down at it, I could only see an all-consuming hatred. Seeing that I knew what this beast needed was one more ounce of lead. It only took a second for me to place that ounce of lead right in the middle of all that murderous hatred. My bullet entered the misshapen forehead, and the damned thing finally stopped moving.

I then ran to the woman and discovered that her skull had been crushed by the blow, or blows, from the monster's bat. I ran back to inspect the creature, one more time. It was naked from the waist down and wearing an 'I'm with stupid' tee-shirt. It was easy to tell this thing was a male because of its, well, you know. The damned thing was hung like a well rope. The creature had one head, two arms, and two legs, but the similarity to man, at least in my opinion, ended there.

This Mag thing looked incredibly strong with muscles everywhere. Wait, that's not exactly right. It didn't look like a weightlifter, it was just, you know, really strong looking. From the body odor and poop stains, it was obvious that hygiene was not at the top of its list of priorities. The one thing about this monstrosity that I still see in my mind's eye were the creature's eyes, the orbitals were squared off rectangles. That fact sits in my memory more than just about anything else. I don't really know why, but those square eyes just creeped me out.

I looked up at the cloud-laden sky, and just at that moment, there came a downpour. I went back inside my house and tried to figure out what the hell was going on, I mean, monsters, ya' know?

Turning on the TV only produced static, so I grabbed my Samsung phone and tried the local radio station that carried talk radio. It was a Conelrad station that was playing a continuous loop, telling everyone to arm themselves because monsters, called Mags, were attacking anyone they came into contact with.

Oh, great, I had survived the sickness that ravaged through town. I lost my wife and nine-year-old son. Both dying early in the plague days.

I spent the week following their deaths crying over my loss and burying them in the backyard. I didn't know what else to do.

Why did they get so sick, that death was their only salvation, while I barely even had the sniffles and some mild congestion? Oh, I also had a pretty bad headache for about a day.

I tried so hard to help my wife and child, but nothing I did made any difference at all. Their deaths came on the twelfth of March. I finally cried myself out on the first of April

My wife and I had a fairly well-stocked food and water supply in the basement, so I felt no desire to venture out of the house. I just sat and cried.

The phones still seemed to be working, well, until around the 15th of March, but no one ever answered, so I continued to sit, cry, and lament my loss in one seemingly never-ending pity party. Whoever reads this should not be judgmental, if you are, well...

Back then I had no idea of the true extent of the impact of this Super-Flu on the world. At that point, I thought that I was the only one to have suffered such a tragedy.

So, I sat, cried, ate, slept, bathed with the rain's runoff into our rain barrels, and just plain felt so sorry for myself that I decided to just wait to die. Maybe then I could be reunited with my family. I even considered suicide, but my Faith told me that I could never end up in the same place as my wife and son if I took that tack. So, I sat and waited for my end. It didn't occur to me, back then, that my plan to just wait for death actually was a form of suicide. I know, bizarre, right?

Anyway, back to the 5th of April. Going back into my home I sat and watched out the window. I saw a few more of these so-called Mags wandering around. They didn't seem to even notice the downpour of rain. Maybe that's how they showered. I don't know, but it could be.

Most were dressed either in pajama tops or tee-shirts. I thought that it was odd that they were naked from the waist down. Watching these monsters stroll around my street like they owned it, pissed me off, but when I saw one carrying a dead dog by the hind leg, I got really pissed. I decided right then and there that I would make it my mission to start taking my street back from these vile things. This is my street, and no monsters are going to take it away from me.

I opened my gun safe and took out my scoped and silenced Mustang mini-24 and all of the 7.62 ammo up to the bedroom and set up a sniper's nest. I'm a pretty good shot, no sniper superstar, but pretty good and from this range of only about seventy-five feet, well, how could I miss.

Over the next twenty-four hours, I knocked off every one of these Mag things that came down the street. Once nine were dead, no more showed up. I guess they got the message, or maybe that was simply all there were on our block. In some, okay I admit, bizarre way, this was cathartic for me, then again maybe it was revenge for my Solange and Christopher, or maybe boredom, hell, I don't know, or care about much of anything right now.

With no more targets of opportunity on my street, I decided to go to my store to resume my revenge mission. I loaded up my car strapped on my .45 and left for a more target-rich environment. I figured that maybe there would be more of these creatures at the Walmart, so off I went. I don't know why I thought that, but I did, and I was right.

-

6 April to 8 April 2118
From the diary of William Bell

April 6, 2118. The Walmart had become a veritable nest of Mags, and I took a great, yet sadistic, pleasure in killing these beasts.

My office has a window that faces the right-side door to Walmart. This became my new sniper's nest. The range was now out to about two hundred yards, still well within range of my Mustang 24.

My goal is for one shot-one kill. Okay, I guess I'm not really as good as I had hoped because, so far, I'm averaging around 1.5 shots per kill. That's not bad, but my ammo is limited to only two more boxes of 7.62 for my Mustang mini-24. If I can kill all the Mags in the Walmart, then I can restock. If not, then I hope they don't find me so I can go elsewhere to find more ammo.

The rain of the 5th had moved on and today dawned crisp and clear. The dust had been washed from the air, which brought a magnificent, crystal-clear morning.

The first Mags began to appear right after sun-up. Once I began firing, they began to scatter. I didn't get them all this morning, but I did get quite a few. It didn't take long for me to realize that there were a lot more monsters than I had ammunition.

Today I shot, napped, ate when the targets stopped presenting themselves; just another day at the office, haha. I'm losing it, I know, and the best part is that I just don't give a rat's ass. I'll keep killing them until they find and kill me.

Late this afternoon I noticed that the Mags have stopped using the front door. Apparently, they have found another way out and have begun searching for me.

It's dark now, and the Mags have settled in for the night...I hope. I've seen them going in, so I figure they don't like being out in the dark. It's funny in a warped sort of way, here I am killing these monsters, yet they may have saved me by giving me a new purpose in life. At first, I thought my street was the issue, but now I realize that these things are everywhere. My street is really the whole country, and I will continue to do what I can to preserve my street, my country."

-

6 April to 8 April 2118
From the diary of William Bell

April 7, 2118. These Mag things have learned to fear my rifle, and they are now being much more stealthy as they search for me.

Oh crap, yesterday, around dusk I may have made the big mistake when I fired one last shot for the day. Apparently, my shot was spotted as I saw one of the Mags pointing in my direction. Oh, man, what have I done? I guess I won't be able to scrounge more ammo after all.

I'm almost out of ammunition, and they definitely know where I am. I'm on my last magazine now with only five rounds left. I do have one, seven round mag for my .45. I figure the end will come in the morning around first light.

-

6 April to 8 April 2118
From the diary of William Bell

April 8, 2118. This will most likely be my last entry. The Mags have broken into the store. They'll soon discover the stairs and come up to find me. I am taking up a firing position at the door, so I can fire straight down the hallway to pick them off as they reach the top. With only twelve rounds left, this last fight won't last long, but I don't plan to have any rounds left when I am finally overrun; one shot one kill, I'll take out twelve more. I hope whoever finds this will continue the fight. This is my country, and it doesn't belong to monsters. It won't be much longer now. I can hear them on the stairs coming slowly up.

Dear God, have mercy upon my soul, and please reunite me with my wife, Solange, and my son, Chris.

"Dear God," were the only words General Merritt could utter. He read the diary entries again before calling in his XO and Staff.

Once everyone was seated around the Conference Table, Major General Tom Merritt read the diary to his Staff. He then said, "XO, I want you to see that every soldier, and I mean every single one gets a copy of this. Also, send it to the Cheyenne Mountain folks for further distribution. I do not want this man to be forgotten. His courage and American stubbornness will give strength to everyone who reads it. Roger?"

The XO looked at the diary and took it from his General with a careful tenderness. He said, "Sir, I will personally see to it that your guidance is carried out. We must preserve this document for the history books."

In the final analysis, the importance of General Merritt's decision to bivouac his troops in the Airport to preclude those who turned from escaping would never be known. Had they been left to scatter, many might have escaped with their weapons, thus increasing the possibility that the Mags would learn to use those rifles for more than clubs.

10 APRIL 2118
WALMART SUPERCENTER
LAGRANGE, GA

Two Ranger Battalions arrived and began to prepare for the kickoff of Operation Trap. They would move south to link up with two battalions moving north from Benning. Small outposts called fire bases consisting of six Rangers, supported by drones would be installed every three-hundred yards along their southerly advance. Outpost number one was named Fire Base Darby, in honor of Colonel William Darby who led Darby's Rangers in WW II. His Rangers morphed into the US Army's modern 75th Ranger Battalion.

10 APRIL 2118
USSDF LEYTE GULF
SPACE FLEET EN ROUTE TO RED SANDS, MARS

The SDF convoy's rate of speed was slow, not due to the convoy itself, but because of the Space Station that was being towed. While it is true that mass has no weight in the vacuum of outer space, it is also true that mass traveling at speed will never slow down. An external counter-force must be applied in direct opposition to the direction of travel. This naturally requires the application of external jets. Unfortunately, the Space Station in tow had no such controls as it was not believed that it would ever leave its geosynchronous orbit above a fixed location. Any alterations to correct normal deviations were made by the station's Space Tugs.

Now, the towed Space Station was traveling at approximately thirty-five thousand miles per hour, with no brakes. Admiral King directed the Stores Officer to issue sufficient portable jets to Engineering. These jets would then be strategically placed to allow for a controlled stop and placement in its new orbit around Mars. Unfortunately, the installation of these jets took quite a while to install, by crews working with precision welders while wearing Space Suits.

The Space Tugs would also be moved to the opposite end of travel to apply additional braking and alignment, as needed. Without these Tug Boats, utilizing the small jets alone, which were jury-rigged to the Space Station, would require a significant amount of time to bring the station to a stop. From a position of being dead still, the Tugs would be used to maneuver the station into its new geo-synchronous Mars orbit.

CHAPTER NINE

THE SNATCH

20 APRIL 2118
175TH RANGER HQ
FORT BENNING

General Merritt met with Captain Abraham, 1Lieutenant Storm, their K-9 Scout Russell, and First Sergeant Bill Tomlin to discuss the landing zone in Atlanta and the mission goals. First Sergeant Tomlin joined Jake's force shortly after the umpteenth mission alteration of 15 April 2118. His job was to supervise and coordinate all the administrative functions of a Company First Sergeant. The increase of the Medical Detachment predicated the need to increase Jake's unit from the original vision of a twelve-soldier squad to a platoon, and finally a fully fleshed out and reinforced Company. Tomlin was a career Ranger and had served with General Merritt since he was a three stripe Buck Sergeant.

The group stood around a large sand table mockup of the Atlanta Braves Baseball Stadium.

"Captain Abraham," said General Merritt, "I am most pleased that we have been able to free up sufficient air assets to be able to assign them to you for the duration of Operation Snatch.

"Your team, now known as Abe's Avengers, cute, but for military records will be designated Easy Company, (Provisional), 175th Ranger Battalion, Special Mag Operations Group, (SMOG).

"My concept and guidance for this mission is for an advanced party of two platoons departing two hours before the main body of Easy Company begins movement to the Braves Stadium.

"The advanced party will have the initial mission of clearing and securing the five stadium entrance gates. Prefilled sandbags will arrive with the advanced party via CH-47. Sandbags will be used to reinforce the gate areas. Both prepositioned explosive devices to be used as a last resort to preclude the loss of any entrance. Claymore mines will also be positioned to repel any Mag attack. These positions will be secured prior to opening the staging area for the main body's arrival.

"The Second Platoon will be dispatched in fire teams to clear the inside stadium areas. Once the stadium is secure, hummingbird drones will be sent to scout out and identify the nearest Mag nest. Following the drone recon's nest discovery, you will make your way to the nearest, cleared upper floor to establish an observation post where you can begin your study of Mag behavior. Any questions, so far?"

"Yes, sir, from your extremely detailed guidance, I must ask; am I in command of Easy, or am I acting as your surrogate Platoon Leader?"

"Jake," smiled Tom Merritt, "what you have just received from me are guidelines. I see your point and can only offer that I am as new to this General thing as you are to being a Captain. Jake, this is your Company and your mission. We good?"

"Thank you, General, we're good. I just needed to make sure that I have the leeway to alter the mission parameters in keeping with any developing situation on the ground," said Jake.

Merritt again smiled before saying, "Jake, complete the mission."

As Jake climbed into the passenger's side of his vehicle, the First Sergeant directed the driver, Corporal James (Oley) Olsen to ride in his carryall. Jake looked over at his First Sergeant and asked, "Something on your mind, Top?"

"Yes, sir, I just want to make something clear to you. First, I have never heard anyone speak to the General like that, and I've been with him for many years. His response to your surrogate comment was not what I would have expected, so I figure he holds you in high regard, and if he does, then so do I. Captain, don't worry about Easy Company, if you'll let me, I'll take good care of it, and make you look good at the same time. General Merritt didn't pull my name out of a hat, so let me do my job, and you focus on completing your mission. Deal?"

"Top, I never thought it could work any other way. So, yeah, deal."

The conversation then shifted to Easy's movement to Atlanta. Tomlin asked, "Sir, what changes to the General's guidance have you already decided on? I'd like to hear your thoughts to see if we're on the same track."

Jake now became the Commander speaking to his First Sergeant, "Top, I have to know something right now. Are you my partner in this fustercluck, or are you the General's spy?"

"That, sir, is the best and most professional initial question that you could ask, and my answer is as follows; I will have no communication with the General without your approval. All communications will go through you. Oh, yeah, Captain, the General has not said one word to me about my reporting to him on your performance, so, yes, we're partners."

"Well, all right, Top, then we are good to go, and I thank you for your candor. It is absolutely true that no man can serve two masters."

"First Sergeant, at this exact moment I have no plans to deviate from the General's Guidance. I guess it just sounded a bit too polished. Maybe he was just being Ranger Tom, or perhaps he was testing me, who knows? At any rate, I kind of like almost all of his guidance, but come to think of it, I think we'll rely a bit less on boots on the ground and more on birds in the air when we search for a close Mag Nest. Your thoughts on that?"

Before answering, Tomlin paused for a few seconds as he took in what Jake had just told him. He finally said, "Well, first off, about the guidance, I think he was being both Ranger Tom and being a bit more in depth because of your level of experience. Secondly, I like your idea about reining in the boots on the ground, yeah, good plan, sir."

This brief feeling out discussion became the beginning of a truly lasting partnership that would evolve into one of deep, mutual respect. The helicopters, ferrying operation, transporting Captain Jacob Abraham's Easy Company from Fort Benning to Atlanta went flawlessly, thanks to First Sergeant Tomlin.

21 APRIL 2118
CHEYENNE MOUNTAIN
COLORADO

As President Holcomb entered the Conference Room, the attendees rose from their seats until he was positioned before his chair. Vance Holcomb said, "Please be seated."

Protocol was now more important than at any time in American History for, without certain protocols and courtesies, contempt and dissension could more easily grow from discussion to revolution and anarchy. The William Bell diary had made its way to President Holcomb's hands two hours before a scheduled meeting with his Cabinet.

"Good morning, everyone," said the President. "I hope you all slept well. My friends," said Vance Holcomb, "the number one agenda item for this meeting is the dissemination of the diary of Mr. William Bell to every American. This man survived a tragedy that every American has also suffered. William Bell fell into a deep depression following the loss of his wife and child, but managed to pull himself from his, as he so succinctly put it, pity party and took a stand for himself, his lost family, and his country.

"It is true that we, as a country, are now on our knees, but the spirit of Bell cannot, must not, be lost or forgotten. One of our Founding Fathers, Thomas Paine wrote a pamphlet called Common Sense which inspired the creation of this nation. Now, a young father has recorded his survival story along with the last four short days of his life.

"This diary will inspire and guide American survivors of the Holly Thorne Pandemic to rise up to defeat this Mag infestation. The American spirit defined by Mr. William Bell will become the rallying call for a revival of what was once this great nation to return to its former glory.

"I direct anyone who has not, as yet, had the opportunity to read Mr. Bell's diary to do so before the end of this day. Your briefing packets contain a copy. Then, looking down at his briefing agenda, the President said, "General Morse, please update us on the Mag War."

The General stood and said, "Yes, sir," before moving to the large view screen. He pressed a button on his remote, and a series of graphs and spreadsheets filled the screen. As he touched each one, they filled the screen, and General Hank Morse explained the significance of each.

"Mr. President, as you can see, we have instructed our military at every Fort and Base in the U.S. to follow the SOPs learned from the Fort Benning, Operation Trap. Trap is approximately 10% complete. Our forces have linked up from the north and south. They have now changed direction eastward to the Chattahoochee River.

"The advance is not so much hampered by the enemy, as by the huge number of buildings in our path. It appears that in this ninety square mile rectangle we are engaging hundreds of Mags. We anticipate this figure to increase into the thousands before Trap is completed.

"We have also encountered one additional concern which was somehow overlooked during the initial planning phase; basements and sub-basements. Our drones cannot penetrate so deep underground. This blindness has forced us to retrieve maps from the zoning commissions of each city and town to assist us in locating these deep earth cavities.

"The requirement to individually inspect each building with these subterranean features has significantly slowed progress. More importantly, it has also increased our losses by 3%."

"And why is that?" asked the Chief of Staff.

"Well, sir," said General Morse, "it is dark with insufficient operational space for large groups of soldiers to clear. The required flashlights give advance warning of our men as they advance into, what we have discovered are Mag lairs.

"Sir, the Mags seem to have the ability to see in the dark much better than us, and our night vision goggles must have some small light source to operate. In the pitch dark of those underground Mag fortresses, our Tunnel Rats often come under a one or two Mag attack."

"Tunnel Rats?" asked the President.

"Yes, sir, that name comes from the soldiers who went down into tunnels after the enemy during the Viet Nam War, back in the 1960s. Our boys have even adopted the same motto; non-*gratum annus rodentum*," said General Morse.

Everyone around the table looked questioningly at the General who finally smiled before saying, "It's Latin and translates as, *we don't give a rat's ass*. Those guys must have balls of steel, I, for one, am damned proud of them. Oh, sir, one other thing about these men; they are all strictly volunteers."

Continuing with his briefing, General Hank Morse said, "Sir, we now know much more about the Mags behavior and their burgeoning skills. We have discovered that they are far from stupid. They have already learned how to use knives, machetes, and the bow. They also outnumber our force by a factor of nearly five-hundred to one. This will, of course, be pared down a bit by the civilian defense forces which are growing each day. Still, the numbers are staggering. My biggest fear is that the Mags will learn how to use firearms."

The President interrupted, "Hank, guns? Really?"

"Sir, I don't care how farfetched that may sound, it doesn't change the simple fact that they may well acquire that ability. These creatures are learning and adapting. Without our opposition, it may have taken them forty-thousand years to achieve a level of technology equal to ours, but with that technology on display, their progress is, well, sir, it's frantic.

"Currently, our estimate on eliminating the Mags in North America is daunting in the extreme. Just eliminating them here in the U.S. could take years. Canada, Mexico, well, maybe the Intel Briefer can shed some light on that."

General Morse then turned the continuing military portion of the briefing over to Admiral Huxley.

"Mr. President, our ocean-going Navy, sans Subs, are now in ports, and, well, sir, there just aren't sufficient personnel to operate them, much less maintain anything larger than a coastal patrol."

Rudely, the FEMA Director, Mr. Norman Freeman, interrupted, "Admiral, why can't you simply combine the survivors from other ships to crew, at least, some of our capital ships; if we need them, that is." His words came out as though he was speaking to a petulant child.

Admiral Huxley was neither intimidated nor was he pleased with the insolent tone of Freeman. In response, Huxley said, "Freeman, I suppose that you would like cooks or perhaps the laundry detail running the critical departments aboard an Aircraft Carrier. Dear God, you are such an idiot!"

The Chief of Staff intervened before things got out of hand. "Gentlemen, we are all under a great deal of stress here, so let's all just take a deep breath and bring the animosity down a few notches."

Mr. Freeman started to rise from his chair in an effort to gain the upper hand in case things did get out of hand. Before he got more than six inches, Admiral Huxley said, "Freeman, do you think you would make it out of that chair before I put you in the ground?"

Then turning to President Vance, the Admiral said, "Mr. President, please accept my apologies for my outburst. I assure you that such an incident will not repeat itself."

Freeman said, "I also regret my actions." There was no apology in his statement, but it did calm things down just a bit.

The President simply shook his head before saying, "All right, can we please get on with the briefing?"

"Yes, sir, of course. The Space Force will attain Mars Orbit on or about April 25th. Admiral Perry informs me that the plan is to present your special orders to the Colonial Governor on the following day. Once that meeting is concluded, Mars will no longer be a Colony; they will be a full-fledged independent Republic. Mr. President, this concludes my portion of the briefing."

Vance Holcomb thanked General Morse, and Admiral Huxley then turned his attention to the CDC.

"Dr. Deen," asked the President, "pray tell, what good news do you have for us?"

Deen said, "Sir, as always seems to be the case, I have both good and not so good news. Sadly, we have not, as yet, even been able to identify this virus, well, we believe it is a virus.

"There is, however, some good news. We have been able to capture two males, and the information we are gleaning from these two creatures is staggering. We know how they initially devolved and the stages of that devolution. In fact, sir, they are still not finished in their change to Cro-Magnon.

"The clothing worn by one of the captured males was much larger than we would have expected. The Mag must have been somewhat obese before the change, yet, in some still unknown way, that fat was transformed into muscle, and in only four days. The possible ramifications for future study are fascinating.

"As you know, we take hourly air quality tests, and to date, we have seen no deterioration in the parts per million of the Mag-Flu. Mr. President, going outside is most definitely not advised."

"Thank you, Tyler. Mr. Freeman?"

With a somewhat bitter, or perhaps arrogant smile, Freeman said, "Yes, Mr. President. To date, we have been unable to make any progress with a census. The only civilian contacts we have are from HAM Radio operators, and they also have no clue about survivor numbers. We shall, of course, continue in our efforts to make headway on your guidance."

"Thank you, Norman. General Morse, perhaps our military could be of some assistance to Mr. Freeman."

General Morse, who intensely disliked Norman Freeman said, "Yes sir, I will instruct each commander to begin a database of survivors. I think we could provide weekly numbers for Mr. Freeman's calculator." He made this statement without once looking at the FEMA Director.

Freeman's face took on a sour expression as he said, "Mr. President, I do not think that we need the help of the military on this issue…"

Holcomb interrupted, saying, "Really? You don't seem to have made any grand strides to date, or have I missed something? Norman, you stated that you do not think, rather than believe. I must say that I agree with you, in that you don't think. Your obvious hatred for our military is beyond the pale…"

Freeman stood, saying, "Mr. President, I do not have to remain here taking such abuse. You will have my resignation within the hour."

"Excellent choice, sir, your resignation is duly recorded in the minutes of this meeting. I accept your resignation with prejudice and absolutely no regret whatsoever at your departure. You are excused. Good day, sir."

And with that, Freeman, who was somewhat stunned that, under the circumstances, President Holcomb would actually accept his resignation, left the room in a huff.

Norman Freeman was a holdover from the previous administration, and because of this interaction, the President asked his Chief of Staff to remain after the briefing to discuss a replacement.

25 APRIL 2118
BRAVES STADIUM
ATLANTA, GA

Jake decided that he, Gale, and Russell would fly into the landing zone with the Security Force, much to the chagrin of First Sergeant Tomlin, who was needed to ramrod the loading and movement of the main body to Atlanta.

"Sir," said a concerned First Sergeant, "I am not, at all, happy with you going in with the security folks to establish the perimeter. We haven't even been able to utilize drones to inspect the area. Captain, are you sure I can't talk you out of this foolishness?"

"Top, I believe that a commander leads best who leads from the front. I know, it's possible that I'm stepping on my pecker with golf shoes, but I am goin' in….tell you what, Top. I'll observe the operation from the air, and we'll land five minutes after the security force goes in and the equipment has been off-loaded, deal?"

"Okay, sir, I like that, and I like the lead from the front stuff, but please, do me a favor, huh?"

"Sure, Top, what's the favor?" asked Jake.

"Just don't get your head bashed in. I'm havin' a hard-enough time breakin' you in, so I don't want to start from scratch with your replacement. Oh, yeah, and don't you dare get LT Storm or that dog hurt, sir."

"Deal, Top, I'll see you in a few hours," and with that Jake boarded the chopper and departed for Atlanta. The Rangers had thoroughly studied the layout of Braves Stadium and three-man teams were dispatched to secure the five known entrances of the field.

The landing went smoothly, as all the Rangers and their equipment were off-loaded. However, once the choppers were out of sight, hundreds of Mags poured out of the entrances leading onto the field.

Ten members of the security team were working to close to the underground entrances to the field and were quickly overwhelmed. The Rangers at once took up positions and began firing on the emerging enemy. The howls of the Mags as they rushed onto the overgrown field would have frightened many a young soldier, but these were not soldiers just out of training. No, these were Rangers. They stood their ground in the face of this terrifying assault. The fight lasted only a very few minutes, and no Mags got closer than ten feet from any member of the Security Force. The Rangers suffered no further casualties. History, however, would record this as the second worst day for military casualties since the Mags appeared as the Ranger losses topped 6%.

Jake watched the surging force of Mags rush onto the field and immediately called in four Dust-Offs to remove the Ranger casualties. Following the fight, a new problem reared its ugly head. What to do with the hundreds of Mag bodies that now littered the field? Jake placed a call to General Merritt requesting CH-47s with sling attachments to be brought in to remove the bodies.

General Merritt said, "Of course, Jake, they should be back on site in minutes. What are your plans for the bodies?"

"Thank you, sir. Once the bodies are sling-loaded under the Chinooks, they will fly ten miles offshore and dump them in the Atlantic Ocean. I'm sure the sharks will appreciate the free meal."

"Good plan, Jake. I'm sorry to hear of your losses, but sometimes good men are simply out of position, with no time to react. Do you have plans for those entrances?"

"Yes, sir, I intend to blow them to block the entryways. I see no reason to ask any of these fine young warriors to go down underground unless it is absolutely necessary, and this time it is not necessary. Sir, I am proud to tell you that within minutes, every Ranger in the company volunteered to go underground to kill those bastards.

"Oh, sir, could you send a few electricians and a couple of dozers with those Chinooks? We should get the sprinklers turned on to soak the blood into the ground."

"Roger, Jake, they're on the way."

"Thank you, sir, if there's nothing else right now, would you please have your commo guy patch me in to First Sergeant Tomlin. I think we will delay the arrival of the Med Detachment until we have things a bit more cleaned up."

"Roger, Jake, here's the Radioman."

25 APRIL 2118
JAKE'S CREW
ATLANTA ZOO

It didn't take long for the drones to find a Mag nest. One flew over the Zoo and immediately spotted several Mags actually tending to the surviving animals.

Both Jake and Gale wanted to run to the zoo, find a vantage point and begin their studies. Unfortunately, for them, that was not going to happen as quickly as they had hoped.

A recon patrol was formed to move out after dark and scout the way to the potential observation post. The drone videos suggested what appeared to be an excellent site on the third floor of a building overlooking one of the open areas of the zoo.

The scouting party returned at 0230 hours on 26 April 2118. Sergeant Jack Rainier reported his findings to Colonel Abraham's team and First Sergeant Tomlin. He also had a pleasant surprise, "Sir, we can have you on the site and doing whatever it is you do within thirty minutes. I suggest you spend tomorrow putting together your supplies and any other gear you may need, and we will get you on site by 0100 tomorrow night.

"I also recommend that we establish two nearby Reaction Teams that can get to you in a matter of minutes. The route to the Zoo provides ample places for the RFs to remain hidden until you are ready to return to Home Plate, or you need a quick extraction."

"Sergeant, I like the plan. First Sergeant, please arrange for our necessary equipment to be ready for departure at 2400 hours."

Turning back to Sergeant Rainier, Jake asked, "Sergeant, get together with the First Sergeant and prepare a list of personnel and equipment you'll need to get us on site to set up the RFs. That is, if you want the job?" smiled Jake.

"Want the job, sir, if you gave it to someone else, I'd be really pissed. Yes, sir, of course I want the job. Top, when would you like to go over my lists?"

First Sergeant Tomlin said, "0900, Tiger and don't be late."

"No sweat, Top, see you at nine."

Once Sergeant Jack Rainier was dismissed, Captain Abraham and First Sergeant Tomlin looked at each other and in unison said, "Promote him."

25 APRIL 2118
WALMART,
PRESCOTT, AZ

The General Manager of the M&K Gun Sales heard the KFNA Broadcast and called DJ Foote. "DJ, it's Andy Baylor, man, it's good to hear you made it."

"Andy, same here. We need you, my friend. Are you able to help arm and resupply our Various Prescott Militia Companies? We have now occupied every Walmart, Target, Costco, and small gun store within a twenty-five-mile swath from Prescott to Chino Valley and out to Dewey-Humbolt. So far, we're doing well, but we need more weapons and ammo."

Andy said, "Yes, of course, but I will need some security and labor to get to the store and load up your trucks. Just tell me when you can fill those needs, and we'll get her done. DJ, we have hundreds of weapons of just about every sort and a huge ammo supply. So, if you have the people, I'll supply the support."

"Andy," said an excited DJ, "if you were here right now, I'd kiss ya'."

Andy laughed and said, "Well, then I'd better shave extra close today in case we meet up."

After the two men stopped laughing, Andy asked about this Colonel Sharpe. "Does she really know what she's doing," asked Andy.

"Oh, hell yes. She's a career Army Gunship Pilot with, I think it was 11 combat deployments. I'm tellin' you, Andy, she is a regular Joan of Arc. The troopers would follow her anywhere. Don't you worry, she will lead us to the end of this Mag bovine scat."

"Bovine scat?" asked Andy, "Oh, wait, never mind, Bovine Scat is BS. I'm glad to hear that you haven't lost your sense of humor."

"Not bloody likely," chuckled DJ, "but seriously, we are lucky to have her…very lucky."

Andy was thrilled to hear his old friend offer such high praise for Colonel Sharpe.

"Say, DJ, what do you hear about the rest of the country."

DJ told Andy that things were not good elsewhere. "At least here in the U.S. we are fighting back, but there are just so many of them. It's not that we don't have the people willing to man-up, it's the shortage of ammo. People everywhere are running out, and once they do, those Mag bastards just run over them. Now that the food in the big cities is running short, the Mags are moving out into the rural areas by the millions.

"The military is trying to pass out weapons and ammo as quickly as they can, but the shortage of pilots and supply folks is making for tough going. We heard a broadcast from Cheyenne Mountain telling folks not to stand and die, but to fight a delaying action as they make their way to any of the hundreds of roadside resupply points. To make that stand to the last round is a bad idea. Hell, Andy, I heard that our military is down to only about one-hundred thousand or so."

"Holy, crap, is it really that bad everywhere?"

DJ exhaled and said, "Andy, except for places like Israel, Switzerland, Afghanistan, and Yemen, the Mags rule the roost."

"Wait," interrupted Andy, "did I just hear you say, Yemen? Why Yemen?"

"Andy, Yemen has more guns than people, but from what I can glean for worldwide shortwave, the Yemenis will eventually starve right along with the Mags."

"Oh, man, say, what about Canada and Mexico?"

"Mexico is off the air, and Canada is fading fast. Come winter, the Canadians will be dead, and millions more Mags will try to move south. At least our border with Mexico is walled off, but the desert would also help to keep the Mags from moving north. No, they'll move south to more suitable growing conditions. Still, I'm grateful for that beautiful wall.

"Places like Fort Bliss are being abandoned because there is just no food for the troops. They are moving north to places like Arkansas. The best climates are on the coasts, but that is also where most of the Mags are. It's bad man, really bad."

"Wow," said Andy, "I guess we should be really happy we live here in the Prescott Basin. I don't think we'll get any wandering Mags being a mile high, surrounded by deserts and granite mountains. Brother, with your help, I'm pretty sure that we can get rid of these Mag Ass Hats, we'll be one of the safest places in the entire world."

"That, my friend, is exactly right. With the population reduction, we have plenty of water and a good growing season. Andy, I have to tell you that your call has come at a really good time. Hang on a minute and let me get Colonel Sharpe on the line. You two need to talk and arrange the meetup. I mean, this, Andy, you may have just saved the day. Hang on, I'll be right back."

Andy could hear DJ opening the door to his broadcast room and call for Colonel Sharpe.

25 APRIL 2118
FORT WEATHER

Lieutenant Colonel Eugene Porter arrived with a cadre of Officers and NCOs, along with a Platoon of Helicopter Pilots and Maintenance Personnel. Upon arrival, the new Commander of Fort Weather ordered his Sergeant Major to organize the military survivors into squads, platoons, companies and a battalion HQ.

The surviving senior civilian, Secret Service Agent Leland Ball had functioned as temporary commander until proper military leadership arrived.

The senior military person was Corporal Steve Woods who had assisted Agent Ball in maintaining order. During this period there had been no desertions. Agent Ball informed Colonel Porter that this was the direct result of Corporal Woods' excellent leadership. Woods had taken on the role of First Sergeant.

Following the meeting with Colonel Porter, the civilian personnel were flown back to Fort Benning for reassignment.

Following a conversation with Major General Merritt, Corporal Woods was called into the Colonel's Office which had been the former President's Office Suite. The battalion XO, the Sergeant Major, and the Alpha Company Commander were also present.

As Corporal Woods entered the Colonel's Office, he was surprised at the attending brass but managed to hide his emotion and reported directly to the Battalion Commander, Lieutenant Colonel Porter.

"Sir, Corporal Steven Woods, reporting to the Battalion Commander as directed," said the Corporal in a sharp staccato voice as he saluted Porter.

Porter returned the salute and asked Woods to take the empty seat in front of the commander's desk.

"Corporal Woods," said Colonel Porter, "I have called you here for this interview based on the reports of Agent Ball on your role as acting First Sergeant caused by the lack of any senior military personnel following the battle for Mount Weather."

"Yes, sir," said Woods.

"Upon his recommendation, and via conversations with your peers, I asked Major General Merritt if you might receive a merit-based promotion. I am pleased to report that he has allowed me to make any promotions that I believe are appropriate. Unfortunately, there is a conundrum that I am having difficulty in justifying." Porter hesitated and looked at Woods.

"Yes, sir, may I inquire as to that conundrum?" asked Woods.

Colonel Porter looked at Woods and said, "Son, you have done an exemplary job functioning as the First Sergeant since the 5th of April. The problem for me is simply that at the young age of twenty-three I cannot, in my mind, justify promoting you to that exalted rank.

"After consultations and a consensual agreement with those present, I have decided to promote you to the grade of 2nd Lieutenant. You will take command, under the tutelage of the Platoon Sergeant, of the 1st Platoon of Alpha Company. Your thoughts, LT?"

Woods was stunned beyond his ability to say much of anything for a few seconds. When he found his voice, he said, "Sir, I don't quite know what to say, other than perhaps it is kismet of a sort. I finished my Associate Degree through the University of Maryland last semester and had planned on applying for Officer's Candidate School before all this craziness started. Sir, I don't know how to thank you, and, well, everyone here for believing in me, so yes, sir, thank you, sir."

The 79th Ranger Battalion, posted at Fort Weather stood at attention as the Sergeant Major said, "Attention to orders!"

Sergeant Major read the promotion order confirming that Corporal Jackson Woods was promoted to the rank of 2nd Lieutenant in the Army of the United States of America. Following this the Colonel and Captain Walsh, the Alpha Company Commander removed the corporal pins from

Woods' uniform and replaced them with the gold butter bar of a 2nd Lieutenant in the Army of the United States.

Once the ceremony was complete, the Sergeant Major said, "Congratulations, LT Woods, now as soon as we get outside, tradition dictates that you will receive your first salute from me. I will return it, and you will then owe me one silver dollar, payable upon your finding one."

Lieutenant Woods said, "Sergeant Major, since my plan was, to one day, get to OCS and receive a commission, I already have that silver dollar in my wallet as a reminder to stretch myself to reach my goal of becoming commissioned. Sergeant Major, I would be honored for you to receive my first salute." Woods then reached into his wallet and produced an 1861 silver dollar before saying, "It's yours, just as soon as I get my salute." The laughter was loud and long. Colonel Porter said, "I think you'll do, LT, yes, I think you'll do."

CHAPTER TEN

The Zoo

After arriving at the Zoo Blind, Jake first directed Plato to make a commo check with Sergeant Rainier before he and Gale spent the following hour organizing themselves in their observation blind.

The plan was to then get a few short hours of sleep, but try as they might, sleep evaded their efforts for another hour. The excitement of actually witnessing a Cro-Magnon encampment with live Mags, rather than digging up old bones made sleep difficult to come for either of them, but Russel, the laid-back K-9 was snoring before the gear was even laid out.

The Mags began to stir along with the rising of the sun. "Jake," exclaimed an excited Gale, "this is amazing. Again, we have viable and specific evidence of ancestral memory. I mean, we've known for perhaps a hundred years that Cro-Magnon had begun permanent settlements in the latter stages of their run as the dominant human species. We know they grew wheat, kept sheep, goats, and pigs."

Jake, who was equally excited also commented that animal husbandry went back in time for, at least, fifty-thousand years.

"Gale, what we have here is a living, breathing laboratory of a Cro-Magnon encampment. Plato, access a database on the physical characteristics of the Cro-Magnon. There are some interesting traits I'd like to check on."

Almost immediately, Jacob was able to see a re-creation of the anthropological makeup of the Cro-Magnon Man. Plato had given him a couple of pages on what was thought to be the appearance and lifestyle of the Mags. Jake recorded his thoughts on the metamorphosis from Man to Mag.

It appears that the transformation takes considerably longer than just four days, as initially thought. We have noted that the bodies of the Mags are still in varying forms of transition.

Their bodies and skull formations are slowly becoming distorted, no wait, make that, still devolving into the bone structure of the Cro-Magnon sub-species. There have been discernable changes in body and facial features since our arrival, four days ago; at least in those I have recognized from their attire.

From their clothes, there seems to be no question that Mags come from every walk of life. I've even seen soldiers and clergy. We have recorded a video showing that the Mags have managed to remove their lower garments. Our estimate is that sanitation and hygiene have made this a necessity.

My initial theory is that when they sleep, the bones somehow soften to allow for the continuing change from Human to Mag. Their faces are definitely becoming more square along with a developing slope to the progressively expanding brow ridge. Even the eye-sockets have become squared, no wait, make that more rectangular in appearance.

For three days Jake and Gale made notes and recorded videos of the Cro-Magnon living in this pastoral setting. They were tending some Zoo animals and using others for food. Females were preparing a field for planting, though neither Jake nor Gale could imagine what they intended to grow.

Jacob began a final subliminal recording to his Artificial Intelligence partner, Plato, "Plato," said Jake," you awake?"

Yes, Jacob, really, you know full well that I am always here, and, with baited breath, I await your every command, replied a somewhat snarky Plato.

"Dang, son, did you get up on the wrong side of your algorithm this morning, or are you just hungover?" smiled Jake.

Jacob, please belay your feeble attempts at humor. You know full well that I do not have a humor chip. Jake could swear he could feel Plato's smirk. "Okay, okay, no need to get snippy. It seems odd that you don't have a humor chip, but you must have the cranky version. Okay, Plato, time to get serious so listen up; record our location and make a visual of the surroundings. I'll look out the window so you can see the Mags wandering around the encampment."

Done, oh my goodness, there are a lot of those ugly beasts, aren't there?

"Yep, there sure are. Keep recording everything, well, everything except when I gotta take a crap, okay?"

Droll, Jacob, very droll, and yes, I'll keep recording, except when you are forced to have a bowel movement.

"Good man, Plato, now, notes to be recorded; We'll remain in place until a couple of hours after dark before we make our way outta here. Easy, Russ," said Jake to his K9 companion, "I see 'em."

When Jake chose to purchase an AI for use as a Secretarial Assistant, he had been asked to select a series of personality traits. The options list was long, and Jake wanted an AI that would keep him thinking and interacting with his new assistant. As a result, he decided on a personality that was mildly aloof, somewhat British in speech patterns, and totally dedicated to fulfilling Jake's secretarial needs, even if Plato could be a bit snobbish and snarky. The banter between them kept Jake's mind active and focused on the issue at hand. Ultimately, however, when Jake needed Plato to knock off the attitude, he used the magic phrase time to focus. This caused Plato to become more amenable and cooperative. Over the years Jake came to realize that he was honestly fond of his somewhat snooty Plato.

Plato patched Sergeant Rainier through. "Sir, we have an excellent opportunity to capture both a child and an adult. If we move in the next fifteen minutes, we can take them both down with the dart guns. What are your orders, sir?"

"Sergeant," said Jake, "go ahead and take them down. Once you have them, pass them off to Reaction Force Bravo. It doesn't look like we'll have an opportunity to grab a young one here. Contact First Sergeant Tomlin and tell him to have a chopper ready to transport the two Mags to the CDC immediately upon Bravo's arrival. Any questions?"

"No sir, I understand that we are to take them down, turn them over to Bravo, then wait for you at this location."

"Roger, we should be at your location around 2330 hours, Plato, send a message to HQ that the primary mission has concluded. We should be able to reach home plate forward by around 2400 hours. Okay?"

Yes, done. I'll let you know when I receive a response. Okay?

"Dang it, Plato, knock off being the crabby, okay stuff. It's just a habit of mine. Let's stay focused, okay?"

Oh, all right. Tell me, Jacob, is it getting hot, or could one of my chips be overheating?

"Oh, hell no! Plato, it is not hot out here, so get your chips under control. Schedule a tune-up for yourself, you know, change the oil, plugs, and kick the tires kind of thing."

Yes, all right, I think you may be right. I've sent a request for an eval first thing in the morning, or whenever you can drag yourself out of bed. And don't you think for one second that I missed your tune-up comment; talk about snarky.

"Okay, okay, I apologize, geez, you're as bad as all my ex-wives. No, don't respond, I'm only kidding, you know I've never been married. I guess I'm just really tired."

Plato immediately halted his bantering with Jake and took on a tone of concern. He said, *Jacob, do you want me to trigger a stimulant injection?*

"No, no stims right now, but maybe in a couple of hours."

Plato had the ability to confer with, and manage, billions of nanobots moving through Jake's bloodstream. Many of these microscopic bots contained highly concentrated stimulants and pain reducers, which they could inject directly into Jacob's brain and bloodstream. Other bots kept Jake healthy and immune from every known disease, except one; the pandemic which had resulted from passing through the tail of the Holly Thorne Comet.

Still, other bots worked to repair damage from an injury, not immediately, of course, but they were able to stabilize most non-lethal wounds and keep Jake moving until he could hopefully get to more comprehensive medical care.

He and Gale had both come through the Mag flu, as it had been named. Jake had suffered mightily, yet Gale had reacted with only a slight head cold. He was convinced that he would not have survived without Gale nursing him back to health. In the six weeks since that freakin' comet passed by he had never heard of anyone being only mildly sick. They decided to keep Gale's case to themselves. Jake definitely did not want her to be carted off to some CDC house of horrors.

Jake began recording a draft consolidation of the four days of notes made by himself and Gale on their observations of Mag behavior.

Initial assessment: at first, we were somewhat surprised that we are seeing far fewer Mags than we anticipated. In 2117 the city of Atlanta and the surrounding areas held a population of nearly fifteen million people. Gale and I believe that we would find few dogs, cats or other animals in the Greater Atlanta Area as they would have been the initial food source of the Mag diet. Now that they are mostly gone, I fear the predominance of the Mag population has begun to move into the more rural areas. With Atlanta's 2117 population we can extrapolate that there would be roughly 1.5 million Mags, but we believe that the total population, still in the Atlanta area to be less than one hundred thousand.

We hear gunshots daily as the local population along with the military from Fort Stewart takes the fight to the Mags. While this is a good thing in many respects, it does not bode well for the more rural areas which will quickly run out of ammunition and be overrun before we can get to them to provide arms and ammo.

Note to self: if most of the world is now populated primarily of these monsters, can mankind ultimately survive?

A shot rang out, three stories below Jake, interfering with his review. He peered out the window and saw a Mag, still wearing the top half of a policeman's uniform, laying on the ground, dead from what surely must have been an accidentally self-inflicted gunshot.

Other, nearby Mags rushed to the downed former cop. One Mag picked up the pistol and began looking at it from all angles. He sniffed the barrel, and quickly pulled his head away from the smell.

As Jake watched, he recorded the Mag holding the pistol. He was mildly surprised at how quickly the creature learned how to properly place it in his hand. Further inspection took his finger to the trigger. He moved the gun around and without realizing how or why, he pulled the trigger, causing the weapon to discharge with a very loud bang and a 9 mm hollow-point round directly into the Mag standing beside him. The bullet struck the left shoulder, spinning him around as he fell to the ground. Other nearby Mags began attempting to assist their wounded brother.

The Pistol Packing Mag stood looking at his mate who was now sitting up and screaming in pain before returning to his inspection of the 9 mm. Within moments the wounded Mag bled out and died.

Jake was most interested in the reactions of these creatures, especially those of the shooter, as he scratched the top of his head and continued to inspect his prize. He soon walked away, still holding his new toy.

Oh, crap, thought Jake, *that one is going to learn how to use that pistol. The only upside is that he will soon fire the remaining twelve rounds and then what? No, he'll associate it with magic and then throw the pistol away, I hope.*

Jake made a mental note that the pistol packing Mag must not escape when the Rangers destroyed this village.

28 APRIL 2118
EAST WYATT EARP RD
DODGE CITY, KANSAS

The clan of twenty-six traveled westward, crossing E Wyatt Earp Road at 11:00 a.m. They had done well since leaving Fort Riley. The small group began as four former soldiers from the 1st Armored Brigade Combat Team, The Big Red One.

The first morning of the awakening had been bitter and bloody as the Mags took a terrible toll of the surprised and disbelieving Human survivors. Yes, the early hours cost the Humans dearly, but within hours they began to rally. Their clubs spat fire and death. By dawn of the second morning, the Mag presence was reduced to a few hundred individuals and small groups. They had gone into hiding as the light began to fade into darkness.

The Mags sought refuge in the darkness, but safety did not come as the Humans continued to search out Mag survivors. A few small bands of Mags fled the fury and unending terror caused by these Humans whose thunderous weapons brought fire and death.

A four Mag clan escaped the fury of the Humans and began making their way west. They chose a westward path as that was the first direction away from the Humans.

Late in the morning of the second day, the Red One Clan was safely away from Fort Riley, they came upon the southern edge of Milford Lake. Here, the forests provided concealment, game for hunting, and fresh water. Two members of the clan wanted to remain in what seemed like the promised land. The leader, a former Army First Sergeant, insisted that they were still much too close to their enemies. The leader thoroughly drubbed the most vocal protester into submission. This action secured the leadership position. The clan moved on to the west.

Within two hours of travel around Lake Milford, the Red One Clan came across three female Mags who were seeking the protection of males. They begged to be added to the Red One Clan. As they continued west, other pieces of ancestral memory kept kicking in. The females were placed in the center of the clan formation to be protected by the males. Hunting was good, and the females knew instinctively how to prepare the ripened winter wheat into a mush.

Red One had picked up other singles, and by the time they arrived at Manchester, Kansas, their numbers had grown to eighteen. Manchester had been a small farming town with a population of ninety-five. The plague had reduced the population to around twenty or so, and by noon of the awakening, the population of Manchester was eight, eight Mags. Their surroundings were familiar, and the area supplied their needs, so they remained. The Red One Clan arrived on 10 April. The leader of Red One wanted a few more in his clan. After killing the Manchester Clan leader, the Mag survivors were incorporated into the Red One Clan.

28 APRIL 2118
ATLANTA ZOO
ATLANTA, GA

The night air was becoming heavy, as storm clouds began to block the stars. Another April Stormfront began to enter the Greater Atlanta area. A moderate breeze was building as it preceded the oncoming rain.

Jake and Gale decided to abandon the majority of the equipment. He would direct the Rangers sent to destroy the Mag Village to retrieve the remaining gear. The combat exoskeleton had taken a bit to get used to, but he and Gale had become comfortable in their use before departing Fort Benning. The suit was lightweight and easy to maneuver. The most difficult part was becoming accustomed to the added strength supplied to the M24-A3, suit, combat, exoskeletal. They both still found it funny to pick something up too quickly and accidentally toss it high into the air.

Jake and Gale were discussing the many opportunities for study that this village presented. Gale wanted to preserve it and study the daily lives of the Cro-Magnon, but Jake stopped that idea cold. He made it clear to Gale that most of the world now had these quaint little villages. He also reminded her of the war which existed between Human and Mag. No, this village would be destroyed by a Ranger Company immediately upon the completion of their mission.

Gale was distressed at this missed opportunity, until she witnessed the return of what could only be construed as a war party. Eight Mags returned to the encampment and each proudly carried human heads. Gale needed no more explanation of the need to rid the world of these vile creatures.

Jacob Abraham and Gale Storm along with the teams Chocolate Lab, Sergeant Russell, sat in their third-floor observation blind. Both watched in horror as the returning raiding party impaled the severed human heads on long poles, near the entrance to the settlement.

They sat in quiet anger, waiting for the sun to set.

29 APRIL 2118, 0030
TWO BLOCKS FROM OBSERVATION BLIND
ATLANTA, GA

Sergeant Jersey Jack Rainier and the two Privates on his Reaction Team moved silently from their security position in a house two blocks from Jake's Observation Blind.

Jack had spotted the two making their way home to the Zoo but being dark they were making every effort to remain hidden. The luck of this apparent father and son duo was about to run out. Being stealthy does not shield one from night vision or Infrared.

Sergeant Rainier would have preferred to take the elder Mag out first, but the critical capture was the kid. He positioned one shooter forward of the Mags as they tried to make their way home. The second shooter remained by Rainier's side in case of trouble from the dart gun, or the dart's potency.

Rainier aimed at the smaller Mag and fired the air gun's dart, hitting the target squarely in the neck. The young Mag roared in pain as he reached for the dart.

The elder, and much larger Mag turned in the direction of Sergeant Rainier and spotting him, roared a challenge and began charging the young Sergeant.

The Private raised his weapon to fire, but Rainier ordered him to hold fire. Sergeant Jersey Jack raised his reloaded air gun and fired at the charging Mag. The dart struck the Mag in the right arm, causing another loud shriek of anger and pain. Still, the Mag ran on and at twenty-five feet away Rainier yelled, "Fire, damn it, fire!"

The Private placed a three-round burst into the chest of the enraged Mag, who dropped nearly at Rainier's feet.

"My God," said the Private while taking a deep breath, "that dart didn't even slow that big bastard down. Did you see that? I mean, holy crap, Sarge, I think I might have just pissed myself."

Sergeant Rainier patted the Private on the back and said, "You did good. I'm glad we both were able to avoid crapping our pants, look at that damn thing. He dropped not four feet from me. Damn good shooting. Tell me, would you have held your fire if I had not given the order?"

"I'm sorry, Sarge, but by the time you yelled, I was already pulling the trigger, and as far as crapping myself? Well, I have to be honest and admit that the only reason I didn't is because my asshole is puckered so tight right now. Hell, Sarge, I may not be able to crap for a week," said the young soldier, as he laughed nervously.

Turning the Mag over, Sergeant Rainier saw that it had been a gang-banger. "Look at this, he has tats all over his face. My man, you not only took out a Mag, but you also bagged a gangsta. Well done, oh yeah, very well done."

The second Private had assumed the role of guarding the younger Mag. As the two Rangers arrived, the Mag began to moan.

"Oh, hell, no!" said Rainier as he jabbed another vial of the sleepy-time drug into the arm.

Both the backup RF and Home Plate had been monitoring the events of the capture. RF 2 arrived and took possession of the captive and made their way back to Home Plate, while Sergeant Rainier's RF returned to their nest to await the arrival of Captain Abraham and his Party.

29 APRIL 2118, 0030
HOME PLATE,
FORWARD TACTICAL OPERATIONS CENTER (F-TOC)
ATLANTA, GA

After four days of Mag watching, Jake was very happy to be back on friendly ground. Even being dead tired, Jake and Gale followed up on the turnover of the two Mags to the CDC. Once the mission was complete and all the data garnered from the last four days was transferred to the CDC, he and Gale made their way to a very comfortable bed; sleep came quickly.

The First Sergeant had ordered that Jake's quarters were established in one of the plush Executive Suites overlooking the field. As Jake drifted into slumber, his last thought was from an old Mel Brooks movie, "It's good ta be da king."

First Sergeant Bill Tomlin ran a tight ship and Rangers expected nothing less, the Med staff, well, not so much. Following the third complaint from Major Stowers, the Med Commander, Jake told him to Ranger up. There would be no turndown service with little chocolates on their pillows each night.

Stowers was furious and quickly contacted General Merritt to complain about a Captain showing such a lack of military courtesy to a senior officer.

General Merritt was not amused at the whining of Major Stowers and informed him, in no uncertain terms, that there would be no mollycoddling. To ease the Major's concern of a lack of military courtesy, the General immediately frocked Captain Abraham to Lt Colonel. Now, Stowers had to make nice with his superior, Colonel Abraham.

30 APRIL 2118
COLONIAL GOVERNOR'S OFFICE
RED SANDS, MARS

The Governor's appointment with Admiral Adolphus Perry was set for 30 April, at 0900 hours. "Governor, Davis? Admiral Perry and Admiral King are here for your 9:00," said Mrs. Tanya Roberts, the Colonial Governor's secretary.

"Ah, good, thank you, Tanya, please ask them in."

Tanya smiled at Governor Davis, then ushered the two Admirals into his Office. Davis stood and welcomed Perry and King as he said, "Good morning, gentlemen. How may I be of service to the U.S. Space Defense Force on this beautiful Martian day?"

The three men sat around a small serving table, upon which Tanya Roberts quickly place coffee and muffins. The three men said their thanks to Tanya, nearly in unison. She smiled and said, "You are all so welcome," as she stood to return to her desk.

"Governor Davis…"

"No, no, interrupted the Governor, please call me Jeff or Jeffrey."

The two Admirals obliged and offered their first names, although King offered his nickname, Sky.

"Wonderful," said Davis, "now, how can Red Sands be of service? Oh, I guess that first, I should ask about the situation on Earth. Please provide any updates you may have."

"Yes, sir," offered Gus Perry, "the situation is far worse than we could have ever anticipated. The Mag-Flu killed over eight billion people, then, roughly half of the survivors of this monster pandemic became monsters themselves. Sir, may I assume that you have seen both the vids from our mining ships and the Mount Weather Facility?"

"Oh, my, yes, dreadful, just dreadful. My staff and I have been racking our brains trying to come up with a way to help. Unfortunately, our limited capabilities and resources make that currently impossible."

"Yes, sir, we understand, and that is why President Holcomb has directed us to request this meeting."

"Yes?" asked a suddenly wary Governor Jeff Davis.

"Sir, President Holcomb, as you know has sent us with a tremendous amount of resources to assist Red Sands in the transition…"

"Transition? What transition? I don't think I follow."

"My apologies, Governor, I guess I got just a bit ahead of myself. I have, with me, a personal letter, addressed to you, from President Holcomb. Perhaps you should read it before we continue with our conversation?"

"Yes, thank you," said Davis as he accepted the letter from the one time most powerful man in the entire Sol System. Davis read the letter three times before he lifted his eyes to his guests.

During the second reading, Davis' right foot began to tap the floor, and before he finished reading the letter a third time his left hand began tapping his cheek in time with his foot.

Davis exhaled deeply and was, for several seconds, without words. He finally said, "Gentlemen, I, I, I," stuttered the Governor, who now was the supposed President of what had, only moments before been a colony. A Colonial Governorship was one thing; the first President of a new nation was quite another. "I need some time to digest the full meaning and scope of this declaration. Perhaps we should schedule another meeting to brief my staff tomorrow morning."

"Yes, of course, I would, however, like to leave you with a breakdown of the assets, both personnel and materiel with you. Everything is on this tablet," which Admiral Perry handed to the stunned President of the new Republic of Red Sands.

CHAPTER ELEVEN

THE REPUBLIC OF MARS

23 APRIL 2118, 0900

GOVERNOR'S CONFERENCE ROOM

RED SANDS, MARS

The three Space Fleet Officers entered the Governor's Conference Room and were introduced to the Governmental Staff. The Governor remained in his office for another ten minutes to allow time for these men and women to get acquainted.

At 0910 hours, Governor Davis entered the room and directed everyone to their assigned seats.

President-*pro tempore* Davis gaveled the meeting to order with three raps on a wooden block.

"Ladies and Gentlemen, we are gathered here to formalize the foundation of a new nation on the Planet Mars. As no name has, as yet, been selected I direct we use Red Sands until a new name for our infant nation can be established.

"You have all received the lists of personnel and materiel that the United States has been kind enough to provide for the creation of Red

Sands. I want it noted for the official record that many items forwarded to us are to be considered as items for safekeeping until the Earthside United States of America has recovered and requests their return. That separate list is also in your packet.

"My friends, in only a few days, Red Sands has gone from a colonial possession to the sole nation on the Planet Mars. as of this moment, I declare that the entire planet is, now and forever, a part of Red Sands."

Some eyebrows were raised at this pronouncement, but there were no objections.

Davis continued, saying, "As the former U.S. Space Defense Force is now the Martian Space Defense Force. I must say that I am extremely pleased to have this addition to our list of assets. Admiral Perry, I now name you as the Supreme Military Commander for the planet Mars, and I charge you with securing your new home, Red Sands, the mining operations within the Asteroid Belt, along with any support the M-SDF can provide our three mother nations."

Admiral Perry stood and while shaking the President's hand, said, "Mr. President I assure you that the M-SDF will offer total loyalty to Red Sands. As you are aware, sir, I have brought with me the Oath of Allegiance to the United States, the United Kingdom, and the Federal Republic of Germany. I hope you will approve the change of names to whatever your people decide to name this nation."

"Thank you, Admiral, I approve your request. Now, moving on, and what an opportunity to excel, we are moving on to. My friends, if we took the time to go over every responsibility for every office and branch of government, we would die of old age before finishing. I, therefore, charge you with proposing your individual areas of expertise to the original Constitution and Bill of Rights of the Founding Fathers of our Mother Country, The United States of America. It is my determination that the law of the land will reside around these two documents. Anything added since the ratification of the U.S. will be placed in abeyance until a need to alter it is absolutely necessary. I would also require you to identify the word Man to be defined as Human. Are there any questions about the direction of this new nation?"

There may have been many questions, but the attendees were so overwhelmed with the task at hand, they were unable to form any intelligent questions, except for one.

"Sir," asked the Colonial Treasurer, "how will we pay for this? Trade with the nations of Earth is now, possibly forever, cut off. From where will the cash come to fund the building projects outlined to speed up such things as terraforming, and the construction of new homes, offices, businesses? Sir, the list is daunting, to say the least."

President Davis said, "Thankfully, because of trade and the acquisition of natural resources, Red Sands has become a rich nation. We are far from impoverished, unlike the U.S. was in its infancy. While it is true that trade with Earth is no longer possible, at least for the foreseeable future. We do have the processing plants necessary to provide the bountiful resources of the Asteroid Belt to build a vast infrastructure to service the future expansion of, not only our fledgling city of Red Sands, but other cities which must be built across this world. We have the technology and the resources to engage in this expansion. To make all this happen, we just have to move that first shovel of sand and never look back.

"A prime consideration here is that we must re-engineer the Earth's carbon dioxide eating moss to assist our fusion powered terraforming generators. If we can manipulate the genes to allow it to survive on Mars, we could conceivably have a breathable Martian atmosphere in another fifty years. "

Addressing Admiral Perry, President Davis said, "Admiral, there has been a theory for the last one hundred years that if Jupiter's moon Europa could be towed into a Mars Orbit of roughly two-hundred-thousand miles from the surface the tidal forces created by Europa and its Magnetosphere could possibly cause significant tidal friction of the Mars core. This tidal friction may cause the Mars core to reheat and begin a rotation. We don't, of course, know if this could actually work, but the premise does have some merit. My question to you Admiral is; is it possible to break Europa away from Jupiter's gravitational pull and place it in orbit around Mars?"

Admiral Perry was stunned by this question and responded with, "Mr. President, that is not a question that I can answer spontaneously. Sir, throwing a lasso around the dwarf planet Ceres would seem more doable and might accomplish the same goal. Why Europa, sir?"

"Good question, Admiral. Even though the Asteroid Belt is only half-way to Jupiter, Ceres is further out of position due to its current point in space. The second reason is that Europa is covered in ice that is hundreds of kilometers deep. That ice, added to Mars ice, is sufficient to provide us with an ocean."

"Sir," said Admiral King, even if placing Europa around Mars is doable, the process will not provide sufficient heat to restart the Martian Core for, well, I don't know exactly, but perhaps thousands of years."

"Yes, that is true. But, if we drill to the frozen core at several strategic points and place nuclear shape-charges sufficient to flash heat the core, the tidal pull of Europa may be adequate to keep the heated magma in motion."

"Wow," said Admiral Perry, "that is an impressive concept, but it does sound quite dicey. Have your scientists worked out the nuclear tonnage necessary?"

"Yes, Admiral, they have. Let's set up a meeting with the team making the plan, say, one week from today?"

"I look forward to it, Mr. President."

President Davis said, "Yes, Mars was a dead planet when we established Red Sands, and internally, this God of War still is. We do have the technology to create a livable atmosphere, and we must move forward in discovering those technologies that will bring Mars back to life. My friends, the road forward will not be easy, but it will be done because the human species and civilization require it."

The meeting lasted for another hour before President Davis set everyone to their many tasks.

30 APRIL 2118
CDC
ATLANTA, GA

Dr. Moishe Feldman literally ran to the CDC Director's office and without seeking permission from Dr. Deen's Secretary, he rushed into Deen's office shouting, "Tyler, I've found it!"

Deen was irritated to see Feldman bursting through his door, but holding his temper, he smiled and asked, "Found what Dr. Feldman?"

The Researcher, nearly out of breath from the race to Dr. Deen's office and the excitement of his discovery managed to blurt out, "Tyler, the turning of the Mags is not caused by either a virus or a bacterial infection."

Deen was now intrigued and said, "Moishe, sit down, take a deep breath, then tell me what you have found."

"Oh, yes, of course, sorry, but I am just so excited. That damned Holly Thorne didn't just bring a disease, she somehow manipulated one ancient strand of human DNA. Like so many other such strands that remain beyond our understanding, it was thought to be just a benign part of our ancestral evolution.

"This one tiny strand of ancestral DNA has come alive and has caused a series of other gene manipulations. I have now isolated that singularly specific gene strand. We can't, at least I don't think we can reverse the effects, but we can correct the problem and make all survivors immune."

Dr. Tyler Deen sat upright in his chair and said in an excited voice, "Gene manipulation, what, how, I mean, oh hell, I'm not sure I know what I mean. All right start from the beginning. Wait, let's get some coffee in here and take a second to relax. I don't want you to leave anything out." Deen called his Secretary and asked her to bring in coffee and donuts.

Feldman took another deep breath and said, "All right, remember Sarah who came to us with the data-pack from the Mag transition?"

"Yes, Moishe, of course, I remember, please continue. No, wait, I need to record this meeting. Dr. Deen then pressed a button that initiated the recording session. Dr. Feldman, you have stated that, though it is still unclear whether the Mag-Flu is actually a virus or bacterial infection that causes some form of gene manipulation. Is this correct?"

"Yes, sir, when Sarah O'Connor first arrived and was put in isolation. She gave us both a blood and DNA sample. Upon examination of her blood, we could find nothing to indicate that she had ever had the flu. Still, we began testing the antibodies from the blood sample.

"I directed the rest of the team to continue testing Sarah's blood. I decided to take a lark and run a series of DNA tests. It took several days before my Assistant, and I were able to discover and isolate one small strand of DNA that was unlike that of anyone else here in the CDC. I know, because I ran cross tests against every person on site, including the two Mags.

"The Mag DNA also showed a mutated strand that was somewhat different from that of Sarah. I have postulated that this tiny Mag variation from the human norm may prove to be the puzzle part which led them to devolve into the monsters they are.

"However, Sarah's mutated DNA strand seems indicative of her saving grace. Like everyone else who has been exposed to Holly Thorne the snippet of that one DNA strand which mutated in one of two ways made all the difference. We don't, of course, as yet, know why this mutation caused roughly one-half of the population to become Mags, while others came through."

"Dr. Feldman," asked the Director, "are we able to create this gene manipulation for anyone who has not been exposed?"

"Oh my, yes. It will take a couple of weeks to work through the process, but yes, it can be done. There is one small stumbling block," added a hesitant Dr. Deen.

A stunned CDC Director, with a sense of urgency, made hand signals to encourage Dr. Feldman, 'Yes, Moishe, go on. What is that small snag?"

"Oh, yes, sir," said Deen, "I apologize. The snag is that the only way to test the therapy, well, when it's ready for testing, of course, is to find three volunteers willing to go outside."

5 MAY 2118
COMMUNICATION CENTER
CHEYENNE MOUNTAIN

The phone rang in General Morse's Office. Hank Morse, the Chairman of the Joint Chiefs picked up the receiver and said, "General Morse."

"Sir," said the General's Secretary, Captain Barnes has asked if you can come to the Communications Center. Admiral Perry wishes to speak with you on a secure line."

"Yes, please tell him that I am on my way."

Four minutes later General Morse was in the secure, soundproof room waiting for the connection with Admiral Perry aboard the MSDF Vessel Leyte Gulf.

A voice came over the line informing Morse that Admiral Perry was on a secure, encrypted call and that there would be no appreciable delay.

Hank Morse heard Admiral Perry say, "Hank, we need to talk, so I'll get right to it. I am aboard the Leyte Gulf and accompanied by Enterprise. We entered Earth orbit thirty minutes ago. Enterprise is currently mapping Mag presence around the Earth. The Captain anticipates that this survey will be complete and ready for downloading to you in approximately seventy-two hours. That, however, is not the reason I am back in Earth orbit.

"Hank, in the weeks before this Holly Thorne mess, the whiz kids at DARPA (Defense Advanced Research Projects Agency) made an AI breakthrough that must not be lost. Their newest version of our AI software allows for instantaneous communication between AIs with have this software update. Hank, I'm not talking about avoiding the booster systems currently in use. I mean that if you have this upgrade, we can speak at any time with no time lapse or signal degradation."

"What? Dolf, did I hear you correctly, unlimited distance and instantaneous communication between AIs?"

"Yes, well, at least within the solar system, but it should be Galaxywide. Einstein provided the basic theory of folding time and space to create instantaneous travel, he said it was like folding a sheet of paper to get from one end to the other without traveling the full length of the paper. Look, Hank, I'm a sailor, not a scientist, but that is the gist of it."

"Yes, I see," said General Morse, I agree, we must find and save that communications breakthrough. I'll get with General Merritt and have him get right on it. Hell, I'll have him bring every computer and every piece of paper in the DARPA files if necessary."

"Excellent idea, Hank. Once you have captured this bit of code, I'm pretty sure I'll have another tidbit of info on this new technology. I hope you don't mind, but I want to prove a theory of mine that may not pan out, so please bear with me. I don't want to say too much about it until I'm sure."

"Of course, Dolf, I'll get right on this. Wow, what a concept, and if it actually works, we'll have an incredible opportunity, here. Look, if you don't have any other fantastic revelations for right now, I'd better get to work on saving that new tech."

"No, Hank, nothing more for right now. I'll get with you as soon as the mapping of the Mag occupation is complete: out, here."

5 MAY 2118
HEADQUARTERS BUILDING
FORT BENNING, GA

Following the communication with Admiral Perry of the Mars Space Defense Force (MSDF)General Hank Morse immediately contacted General Tom Merritt at Fort Benning.

"Tom," said an excited General Morse, "I have a most important mission for you that must be accomplished immediately."

"Yes, sir, and what must I do?"

"Tom, I can't go into much depth here, so please don't ask too many questions. You are tasked with sending a Ranger Company as a security force to DARPA at 675 North Randolph Street, in Arlington, VA. You will also need to send a major detail to do the heavy lifting. The mission is to recover every computer, storage cube, every filing cabinet, notes on desks, wastebaskets, hell, anything that has writing or typing. I don't know how you might find them, but if you can find any of the scientists or computer geeks, take them with you back to Benning.

"What we are looking for specifically are the data cubes storing the latest Personal AI updates. That's all I can tell you right now, but at least you will know the primary mission goal. I hope you have some good cyber guys still alive at Benning, because, Tom, this is really important. I promise to put you on the top of the loop as soon as the President approves. Are you with me, here?"

"Yes, sir, of course," replied General Tom Merritt. My mission is to secure the DARPA complex in Alexandria in Virginia and take everything back to Benning. I'll have everything set up in a secured hanger and get our cyber guys, and we do have seven of them remaining, working on finding the data and codes for the latest Personal AI updates. I think I'll send Lt Colonel Abraham to supervise the collection. He just finished up a major mission for the CDC and is ready to get onto the next thing."

"Tom, did I hear you say, Lt Colonel Abraham? I thought he was a Captain."

"Oh, yes sir, I frocked him to LTC to get a Doctor, a Major, in line as to who was in charge of the mission."

"I see," said Hank Morse, "good thinking. Are you going to go ahead and promote him?"

"Yes, sir, I think he is a real asset, and as an LTC he won't be getting that kind of flak from anyone else. Do you approve?"

"Of course, I approve. Tom, I told you that you have the go-ahead to promote whoever you need to fit into the puzzle. Speaking of which, how is your command structure shaping up?"

"Sir, I think it may be too early to tell, but we'll make it work. Oh, and please tell the Prez that Operation Trap is proceeding nicely. I have to tell you, sir, those Tunnel Rats are making quite a difference in our progress. This might surprise you, but we have more Rangers volunteering for Tunnel Rat duty than we need. My guess is that since our new Army is light in the leadership department, a willingness to go down into those dark assed places may improve their chances for promotion, and they are right. Then again, I, however, choose to believe that they are simply being Rangers. Is there anything else, sir? If not, I'd better get my butt in gear and get the DARPA Mission on the road."

"No, nothing else, Tom, but while your folks are there, make sure they are aware of possible Mag Nests. Our statistics guys tell us that there could be as many as ten-thousand of those ugly bastards still around Alexandria. Oh, wait, one more thing. Tom, keep this under your hat, we are losing this war at present. The Mags are moving into the hinterlands by the millions, and they are consuming everything in sight. If it weren't for your efforts to set up roadside resupply to the locals who are fighting back, it would be even worse."

"Yes, sir, I understand. I think I'll step up the aerial mine laying operations to slow them down."

"Good idea, keep me informed, out, here."

6 MAY 2118
PRESIDENT'S CONFERENCE ROOM
CHEYENNE MOUNTAIN

General Morse and Admiral Huxley requested a meeting with President Holcomb and his Chief of Staff Simon Ward to provide an update on the available military force in the Continental U.S.

The 75" computer screen displayed the Forts and Bases across the nation. "Sir, we have prepared this fact sheet to outline the condition of each military facility. We will, however, focus only on those with an actual, or salvageable, command structure. This slide provides our most up to date status. Mr. President, as you will see, it is not good. Those listed in black had not come back online and were presumed to be total losses.

"Red indicates that there were limited availability of resources but are lacking a functioning command structure. Yellow indicates salvageable command structure and available combat forces which can be brought online for Anti-Mag operation in the next fourteen days. Green displays those Forts which are currently functional and actively engaged against Mags.

"Those areas in black are primarily the smallest facilities, such as Depots, Reserve, and National Guard training facilities. Of the nation's Reserve Forces only a handful have come online, and those have a minimal cadre and a total lack of munitions for their weapons systems. I have directed those Reserve personnel available for duty to commandeer any source of weapons and munitions, such as gun stores. At this point there just isn't much that we can do to provide assistance as they are so few in number and so widely dispersed.

"There are some reports of retired military personnel organizing the local populations into effective anti-Mag operations. Militias across the country are also effectively combating the Mag invasion. Perhaps the most effective of these is in the Prescott, Arizona area where a retired Army Colonel, Cynthia Sharpe has been able to form the Prescott Militia and several spinoffs throughout the Prescott Basin region of Northern Arizona.

"This group seems to be well supplied and very well led. Colonel Sharpe estimates the region will be predominantly Mag free within the next thirty days. We have become aware of the advances in Prescott via a radio station, KFNA, which is the voice of the Prescott Militia. We have also been in contact with KFNA. Their primary needs at this point are the hummingbird drones that we are using across the board in anti-Mag Ops, Like Air Force Base (AFB) made delivery of two-hundred drones, Night Vision Monocles, and uniforms.

"General Merritt is busy meeting with survivor units across the country, in all branches of military service. He is evaluating the available forces and the existing leadership. Tom reports that he is making promotions at every stop, and some of these promotions, both Officer and NCO, go as deep as three ranks.

"He has also ordered a vast expansion of Operation Mine. The Air Force is laying hasty anti-personnel minefields ahead of the advancing Mag invasion. Sir, this effort will not win the war, and considering that we could be looking at, as many as fifty million Mags in the U.S. alone, this effort may not even significantly slow them down. It will, however, whittle them down by some big numbers."

"My God," said President Holcomb, could there really be that many? Fifty million?"

"Mr. President, I am loathe to say it, but our statisticians estimate that of the four-hundred-million Americans, 75% died from the pandemic, and as many as half of the one-hundred-million survivors turned into Mags. Human losses are far greater due to deaths of those over sixty, those under ten, the sick, and others for, oh so many other reasons."

President Vance Holcomb began rubbing his temples, as he often did to try to stave off a looming migraine. "Thank you, Hank, please continue."

"Yes, sir, General Merritt also reports that every large Marine, Air Force, and Army Base and Fort have come online and are currently engaged against the enemy in ops like Trap.

"Unfortunately, sir, the Navy has only one recruit training base. It is located just north of Chicago on Lake Superior. I have ordered that it is to be closed and the personnel there transferred to the southernmost Naval Bases before the coming winter. All surviving Navy Seals have been ordered to provide security and appropriate anti-Mag operations that present themselves.

"Sir, as you can see from this next slide, the true availability of U.S. Military operations against the millions of Mags now swarming across the country is but a very small drop in the proverbial bucket. As our forces expand outward from their home base, they grow ever weaker due to a diminishing supply line. At some point, we will have to go into a holding and consolidation mission, similar to the Western Forts of the late 1800's.

"General Merritt has begun to both create and support militias across the country based on the Prescott model. In this way, a finite number of our military will be available to assist and recruit local forces to fight the Mags.

"The Air Force assures me that they can provide air supply and deployment to these small detachments. Our own Green Berets are highly trained in this exact type of mission. They will be training volunteers in a crash course in militia tactics to include guerrilla warfare.

"Our surviving Special Operations Forces will be used for rapid deployments against Mag concentrations by assisting localized militias when confronted by overwhelming numbers, or a heavily entrenched enemy. As these special ops personnel are distributed across the country, the SOF units deployed will, whenever possible, be those closest to provide the mostest.

"My personal belief is that the Air Force can, certainly, provide this support, at least in the short term. They, like all branches of our military, suffer from a lack of personnel, as in aircrews and support personnel. Add to this the simple fact that the more teams we get on the ground, the more difficult the task of resupply."

President Vance Holcomb said, "Hank, that is one hell of a bleak picture you have painted. Tell me, bottom line, can we win?"

"Sir, these creatures will only win if they can kill every human in uniform, but there is no short-term solution. It will take a minimum of three or four years, and that is discounting the efforts to retake the major cities, like New York. In truth, Mr. President, we don't have even a remote idea of how to retake a city like New York or San Francisco."

"Wait, Hank, didn't you say that come winter the northern states will force the Mags to move south? Won't that resolve the problem, at least with the likes of New York and Chicago?"

"No, sir, I'm afraid that is most unlikely as these cities have huge undergrounds. If the Mags cannot find other sources of food, they will survive on rat meat. This is, of course, all supposition, but it does seem like the most reasonable scenario."

"And the rest of the world?" asked the President as his voice trailed into a whisper.

THE END

TO BE CONTINUED IN *AMERICA FIGHTS BACK*

BOOKS BY CLIFF DEANE
The Vigilante Series
Vigilante: Into the Darkness
Book one
Post-Apocalyptic Justice
Vigilante: Into the Fray
Book two
Post-Apocalyptic Justice
Vigilante: The Pale Horse
Book three
Post-Apocalyptic Justice
Vigilante: No Quarter
Book four
Post-Apocalyptic Justice
Vigilante: The Way West
Book five
Post-Apocalyptic Justice
Vigilante: Indian Territory
Book six
Post-Apocalyptic Justice
The Oort Chronicles Series
Red Alert: Missiles Inbound
A Prelude to Apocalypse
Book 1
The Oort Plague
The Pandemic Apocalypse
Book 2
America Fights Back
The Mag Apocalypse
Book 3

ABOUT THE AUTHOR

Cliff Deane grew up in South Charleston, West Virginia. At 17, he left school and joined the U.S. Cavalry, as a Private. 35 years later, he retired as a Lt. Colonel, spending 10 years Enlisted, and 25 years Commissioned.

Cliff holds a High School G.E.D., a Bachelor of Science Degree in Elementary Education and English, a Master's Degree in Education Administration and Management from West Virginia and is a graduate of the U.S. Army Command & General Staff College.

After retirement, a love of the American West took Cliff to Prescott, Arizona, which he has called home for many years.

Today, Cliff and his dog Katie reside full time in his 44' Toy Hauler. He and Katie just go where the wind blows, as long as the wind blows them to Sturgis, SD in August.

THANK YOU FOR READING!

If you enjoyed this book, we would appreciate your customer review on your book seller's website or on Goodreads.

Also, we would like for you to know that you can find more great books like this one at www.CreativeTexts.com

www.ingramcontent.com/pod-product-compliance
Lightning Source LLC
Chambersburg PA
CBHW030739110726
47900CB00008B/2374